Sing, Little Bird, Sing

Cindy M. Rankin

crippledbeaglepublishing.com
Knoxville, Tennessee

Cover design by Jody Dyer and Cindy M. Rankin

Paperback ISBN 978-1-958533-37-6
Hardcover ISBN 978-1-958533-38-3

Library of Congress Control Number: 2023908546

Printed in the United States of America

I dedicate this book to my husband, Wayne, and to all the good fathers in this world.

Thank you!

A Suggestion from the Author

Go to YouTube. In the search box, type "piano music" for the name of any piece listed in this book. Enjoy the music to get a better feel for the characters and their experiences.

Chapter 1

June 1886

Outskirts of southeast Macon, Georgia

At the end of Pecan Lane was a two story, two-bedroom bungalow with gray wooden siding and white trim. There lived the Rollan family.

Husband George was thirty years old, a white male with short brown hair, brown eyes, medium build and height, and plain looking. He was a traveling salesperson.

His wife Susan was twenty-five years old, a white female, housewife, and mother. She was of medium height and build, with brown eyes, and long brown hair braided down her back, and she was pretty. Susan taught piano and voice lessons at home.

Their daughter was Catherine, nicknamed Kitty. Kitty was almost nine years old, with long, mousey brown hair and large brown, sad eyes. She did play piano, and she played well for her age. She started playing at age two. Kitty did not speak.

This is their story.

On the first Friday in June, at 3:00 PM, Susan and Kitty were preparing dinner. Kitty took a peach pie from the oven and placed it on a counter to cool. Susan placed the last biscuit onto the baking sheet and covered it with a tea towel to rest. Susan handed the mixing bowl, rolling pin, and biscuit cutter to Kitty to wash. She then stirred the stew in the pot on the stove and covered it to simmer until dinner. All was set. They washed their hands and hung up their aprons. “Well done. We will put the biscuits in the oven to bake when George washes up for dinner. We have time until he arrives at about five. Let us look over the new piano sheet music we bought yesterday and see what we can do.”

Both girls wore matching light gray dresses that Susan had made. Yesterday, Susan bought a pink calico fabric to make Kitty a dress with a matching hat for her ninth birthday. She splurged and bought a lovely printed white fabric for a long over-apron and several ribbons. She would work on it at night for the next couple of weeks.

They walked into the living room and sat side by side on the piano bench in front of an upright piano. How they enjoyed playing the piano together. Playing the piano let Susan escape from her troubled reality. Kitty escaped to a magical wonderland when playing the piano. Two of her favorite things, music and her swing, helped her to escape the reality of her situation. Music made her soul and body sing. There were no words for how she felt when she played. They practiced the first line where Susan played the lower keys and Kitty played the upper keys. They practiced until the song was perfect.

Suddenly, the front door banged open. George stood with his briefcase and suitcase under the same arm. He placed both inside and closed the door. "Susan, I'm home early because I have a big surprise!"

Susan got off the bench and went to her husband, talking her way to the door so that Kitty had time to make herself scarce. When Susan got to the front door, she gave George a quick kiss on the cheek. She smelled the alcohol, ignored the common aroma, and asked, "What is the surprise?"

George exploded with joy and blurted, "I have been promoted to manager for the entire state of Florida! I will have an office in Tallahassee. Get ready to move. Tomorrow, I will find a moving company, boxes, and paper so you can start packing. Hopefully, we will move in a week or two."

Kitty's body tensed. The hairs on back of her neck stood on end. She feared what he would undoubtedly say to make her feel small and of no worth. She dared not move but wanted to flee. She felt like a fly on the wall, not wanting to be noticed. She waited for her mother to distract him so she could flee. Out of sight and mind. At that moment, Kitty stood up from the piano bench to escape outside.

George spotted her. "But…" he turned toward Kitty and pointed a finger towards her, "before I get home next Friday, I want her gone! Take her to an orphanage, girls' home, relatives, anywhere! I wanted a healthy boy, but what did I get? Her! A girl who is a *mute*. I do not want to put up with her retarded behavior or ever see her again. She will embarrass me in Tallahassee. Do you understand, Susan?" His blatant demand stunned and rendered Susan speechless.

Hearing this from her father, Kitty ran to the backyard and jumped onto the tree swing that her Uncle Tom had put up for her. No tears came. She was used to his verbal assaults. George was always cruel in his attitude and speech toward her. But in this moment, Kitty felt a new sensation of panic. She felt hopeless. Never had George threatened to separate her from her mother. She felt so rejected and unwanted. She was terrified that her mother would reject her now. Where would her mother send her? Kitty felt so alone.

She knew all fathers were not like hers. Uncle Tom was loving and kind. She wished she had a father like him. She planned to stay outside until her father went to bed. She was always safer and better off out of sight. Tomorrow, she would sleep late until he left for the day. As she swung, she listened and prayed her mother would fight for her.

"But George, she's, our child!" cried Susan.

"She is not my child! She is a stupid girl who humiliates our family! She will be gone. Take care of it, or I will get rid of her myself," George spit out.

Susan bought time. She needed to think. She tirelessly worked to protect Kitty from his outbursts and hateful talk, but now she was worried on a whole new level. She could not be separated from her daughter. She'd rather die. Struggling to keep a calm countenance, she breathed in deeply and said something routine. "Okay, George. Go take a shower, and I will get the biscuits cooking and dinner ready. Again, congratulations." Susan went into the kitchen. Shaking, she popped the biscuits into the oven and stirred the stew.

Once George was upstairs, Susan quickly ran outside. There, swinging with no signs of emotion, Kitty waited. When she saw her mother. Kitty stopped and faced her. Susan placed her hands on each of Kitty's checks and said, "No way am I getting rid of you, my love." Kitty sighed in relief. "On Sunday, we will go to Aunt Carolyn and Uncle Tom's for our regular luncheon. Before lunch, I will discuss with them what is happening while you kids play outside. Hopefully, they may have an idea where we can hide and how to get there before your father gets back. Just do what you always do—stay away from him until he is gone. All will be all right. I promise you. I love you. I will NOT leave you." Susan kissed Kitty's forehead, hoping she was able to reassure her precious daughter.

Susan went back inside to fill only two water glasses, put the biscuits into a doily basket, and carried the waters and biscuits to the table. Finally, she brought the stew to the table just as George began to sit down. They ate in silence. As Susan cleared the table, she realized the man she married was not the man before her. She had had enough of him, and this last demand was her wakeup call. She gave George his peach pie and coffee, then sat to have her coffee.

"This pie is delicious," complemented George.

"Kitty made it especially for you," Susan retorted.

"At least she can cook and clean. I am sure you can find her a position in a kitchen or as a housemaid at least," dug in George with a smug expression. "I am beat. It has been a long day. Tomorrow, I will see what timeframe we have with the movers once I pick one with the right price. Who knows what time I will be back? (Susan knew he would be at the pub drinking all afternoon.) So, do not expect me until dinner or later. Make sure you wash my clothes and repack them. I want to go to bed early tomorrow night so I can get up at dawn Sunday, have breakfast, and leave to find a temporary place to stay in Tallahassee until we move. Monday morning, I will inquire at a bank there to see what properties are available. I will come home and stay overnight Sunday, so I can go to our bank as soon as it opens on Monday, I will meet with the manager to have him list our house for sale, and then I'll head back to Tallahassee to start working."

"All right George. Again, congratulations," Susan replied.

George left, and Susan cleared the dining room table. She went out back to get Kitty. She placed Kitty's dinner on the kitchen table. Kitty ate little as she felt unassured of her life. She could not even touch her peach pie.

"Go to bed, Kitty. Sleep late. After he is gone, we have a lot to do. I love you." Susan kissed Kitty's forehead and sighed. Susan could only think about what she had to do in the next two days. Everything was overwhelming and would be until she talked with Carolyn and Tom. Thank goodness, she and Kitty had a caring and loving family to reach out to for help.

Saturday came at a fast pace of washing, ironing, repacking, and making dinner. Kitty picked out a book to read and other things to amuse her until George went to bed. She placed a sandwich, a glass, a pitcher of iced tea, and her peach pie on the back porch table for later. All was set. Susan called her sister, Carolyn, to let her know they would be coming on Sunday to have a serious talk before their usual Sunday lunch.

Susan knew that after dinner she would suffer through George's disgusting routine of sex, collapsing, then falling fast into a deep, snoring sleep. She would put Kitty to bed, clean the kitchen, then try to get some sleep so she could be ready for Sunday, a crucial and frightening day for her daughter and her.

Chapter 2

George and Susan were up at dawn. She made bacon, eggs, and toast with black coffee for him. He read the newspaper while eating. When he finished, he kissed her goodbye and reminded her of what he expected her to do before they moved.

Once Kitty heard the front door close, she came downstairs for a breakfast of pancakes with lots of butter and syrup along with a large glass of milk. Kitty then went upstairs to dress as her mother cleaned the kitchen.

When Kitty returned, Susan said, "Let us put on our coats and hats before we go to church. The air is a little brisk."

The two were dressed in matching navy dresses, hats, and coats. They looked like twins. Off they walked to church, where they acted as normally as possible during the long service, despite their nervousness. Susan instinctively felt she needed to stick with her routine until she had a plan in place. The peaceful service gave her time to think. After church, Susan and Kitty walked to the Harris house. The weather was sunny, promising hope and a future. They reached the two-story blue with white trim, Victorian, gingerbread house with a lovely, covered porch. They used the door knocker to announce their arrival to Mabel (the cook and housekeeper).

The door opened to a smiling face of a rotund black woman with a large white apron and white, wrapped headdress. “Miss Susan, Miss Kitty, please come in. Let me take your coats and hats.” They handed their items to Mabel. She smelled like baked cookies, which was heavenly. “Take a seat in the living room while I get you some lemonade and a couple of shortbread cookies for Miss Kitty, to tide her over until lunch.”

“That would be wonderful, Mabel,” thanked Susan.

“Folks should be home any minute from their church service. You relax.” Mabel returned with drinks and cookies, then went off to the kitchen to finish making lunch.

Just as Kitty finished her cookies, they heard stomping of feet coming up the front steps. The Harris family had arrived. The boys, Tom, Jr., and Frank, rushed into the living room and yelled, “Hello, Aunt Susan and Kitty!” They gave their aunt a peck on her cheek. “Can Kitty come outside and play with us until lunch?”

Their younger sister, Savanah, followed the boys and gave her aunt a peck on her cheek then asked politely, “Please Aunt Susan. I love to play with Kitty.” The girls hugged. “We have such a great time!”

“Of course,” replied Susan cheerfully, “Kitty, put your coat and hat on before you go outside.”

Kitty nodded. Savanah giggled as the girls went to get Kitty’s coat and hat. Hand in hand, they joyfully walked outside. Susan was thrilled to see Kitty smile for a moment. She felt bad Kitty did not have any friends due to not being able to talk. She was shunned at church and by the neighbors. Kitty communicated with Susan through writing about how she did not feel lonely. She wrote that she had plenty to do with her mom, including with the Harris family and practicing the piano.

Carolyn and Tom hung up their coats and hats. Mabel appeared, and they asked her to keep an eye on the children while the adults had a talk. Carolyn and Tom went into the living room, kissed Susan on the cheek, then sat down in their chairs across from Susan. They were like bookends—tall, slender, brown hair, dark eyes, and attractive. Carolyn started in a soft voice, “Okay, Susan. The children are gone. You sounded awful on the phone the other day, and I know George was in earshot. He's not here, so tell us what is happening."

Susan held back her tears. She needed to get it all out so they could help them. "George is now the manager of all regions across Florida, which means we have to move to Tallahassee. The problem is…" she paused to collect herself before going on. This was the tough part. Carolyn and Tom kept silent to let Susan finish. Susan took a deep breath then shakily continued, "George wants Kitty gone for good." She was embarrassed that she had married (and stayed married to) such a cruel man, but in those days, divorce was scandalous and rare. Both Carolyn and Tom gasped. "He refuses to have her around anymore. I am to get rid of her before he comes home on Friday." Tears ran down her face.

Carolyn jumped up, sat next to Susan, and hugged her. "That animal!" yelled Carolyn in shock.

Once Susan got control of her emotions, she explained, "I must pack up a few things and take Kitty away. I have no idea where to go or how to get there. Can you help me? Please! I have almost no time to figure this out, and I'm terrified. So is Kitty." She cried more then worked to compose herself.

Agitated, Tom stood up and paced for a couple minutes to think and to let Susan calm down. "Let me make a couple of calls. Once I have answers, I will be right back and talk about some plans." The ladies nodded as Tom left for his study.

Cradling Susan, Carolyn let Susan cry her heart out until she stopped and could breathe normally. Carolyn handed Susan a hankie to dry her tears. "It is going to be all right. You know Tom. He will find a way," Carolyn reassured.

Close to an hour later, Tom came back. "Susan, you remember my sister, Ida, from our family gatherings. The one who lives in Marietta, Georgia, and lost her husband and son two years ago?" Susan nodded yes. "She said she would be happy to have you both come stay with her. She is incredibly lonely and will be a wonderful help to you and Kitty. She's very loving. You both will need to invent new names. Ida will tell her neighbors that her sister and niece will be staying with her due to the loss of your husband. Choose a name for Kitty and yourself."

"Kitty loves the name Lily. She will be Lily Mae Faye. I will be Violet Anne Faye."

"Good. You will be coming from Odom, Georgia. No one leaves that small town. Ida was a professional pianist before she met her husband. I told her about Kitty's talent, and she is excited to tutor her. Ida has a small farm where she sells her vegetables, various fruits, and canned goods. She is out in the country. You both will love it and feel safe there.

"Also, I have a good college friend who is retiring from his moving business in Virginia. He has volunteered to come on Wednesday evening while George is in Tallahassee. He will load you up. He will drive you to Ida's, help you move in, and stay for a while to make sure there is no trouble. What do you say, *Violet*?"

"Please give Ida our new names and thank her from the bottom of our hearts. Advise your friend to paint over any signs on his moving truck and maybe paint a fake name in their places. We have nosy neighbors, and this will prevent any links they can use to help George find us."

"Great idea. My friend's name is Duncan McDougal. Also, Andrew Miller is from my office. He will help pack the wagon here. These gentlemen can protect you if needed, especially if George unexpectedly shows up at home on Wednesday. You can trust them. Let me make a couple more calls to confirm everything up then we can have lunch. You will be in Marietta in no time. Trust my sister and God to disguise and protect you. I will have Mabel bring you ladies iced tea." To assure Susan, Tom said, "Okay, Violet?" When Susan nodded at her new name, Tom patted her knees then went to make more calls.

Once all was set, Tom called the children in to wash up for lunch. Mabel had made enough food to feed an army. Mabel prepared a basket of leftovers for Violet to take home, enough for them until they moved so that Violet could focus on packing not cooking. Violet thanked Mabel for her thoughtfulness.

Tom grabbed the basket and said, "I'll drive you home." Once in the motorcar, he continued, "Pack what you only need and leave the rest."

"We really just need the piano, sewing machine with supplies, legal papers, sheet music, pictures, and a few clothes."

"Do you have any money?"

"I've saved some."

"I have money your mother gave me to save for you in case something like this happened. She never did like or trust George. Also, in her will, she left the house to Carolyn, not you, because she was afraid he would put you in poverty and leave you homeless at some point. Fortunately, because I was the executor, I was able lie to George. I told him the house was in your name. I lied to you, too, but only to protect you. If George does sell the house, the truth will come out in the paperwork, and he will not get a cent. We can sell it, but it is best to rent until you either need money, can safely move back in, or eventually want to sell. This way, you will be getting an income to live on, or I can bank it for you. Do you need any boxes or paper for packing?"

"No. George brought those home. He will think I'm packing to go with him and to send Kitty away with her things. Thank you so very much for everything, Tom. I do not know how to repay you."

"Just be safe and have a happy life. That is all we ask." He helped them from the motorcar then hugged both ladies. "Remember, we are always here for you and love you both."

Violet and Lily went inside the house, unpacked the basket, and put the food away. Violet hugged Lily and explained she needed to remember their new names and the plan. They sat down to make a list of what they needed to bring. It was noticeably short. but would still take time to pack by Wednesday. Thankfully, they did not need to worry about cooking with all the food Mabel had packed.

Time would fly by. That night, they both had the best sleep ever and dreamt of good, safe, peaceful lives without George.

Chapter 3

Wednesday afternoon came and plans were set in motion. Violet and Lily sat at the piano and played several tunes by heart to calm their fears that George would surprise them by coming home any minute and ruining their plan. Next, they finished the food from Mabel then cleaned the kitchen. Violet was not leaving anything for George to eat. *He can fend for himself now*, she happily thought.

At 7:00 PM, there was a knock at the front door. Violet opened the door to a tall, blonde, blue-eyed, muscular Scotsman named Duncan McDougal.

"Hello. I am Duncan McDougal. This is Andrew Miller. We are here to help you move."

"Please come in. I am Violet and this is my daughter Lily. She does not speak but understands everything you say. Let me show you what is going with us."

Andrew and Duncan made a list of items to pack. They loaded the sizable items first, then carried out the boxes. It only took about an hour. When all was finished, Violet placed a note to George on the dining room table.

Dear George,

I have just found a place for Lily. I will not be back tonight. I have sold the piano and a few items. You need not worry.

Susan

That should appease him until they were far away and settled, thought Violet.

"Ladies, do you need to use the restroom before we leave?" asked Duncan. The ladies nodded yes. "Ladies, once finished, come sit in the front of the truck. Andrew will sit in the back with the boxes."

The men went outside to stand next to the truck. "I feel sorry for the mother. What a situation! And did you see that child?! She looks pitiful," exclaimed Andrew.

"Tom said with love and help, Ida will make a tremendous change in both. His sister sounds special," Duncan replied. They jumped into the truck and awaited the ladies.

Once ready, the ladies got into the truck. An hour out of Macon, Duncan pulled over. He took off the painted signs and put them in back with the boxes, not waking Andrew, who had fallen asleep. Half an hour later, the ladies, too, fell fast asleep until the sun's rays hit their faces.

"We are close to Ida's house. Anyone need to use the bathroom?" asked Duncan as they were approaching a church on the right.

"We can wait," they both responded.

"Okay. We are just twenty minutes away," explained Duncan.

They soon turned off the major road. On the right side was a directional sign for Clinton's Apple Orchard and Cider Farm, and on the left side was a directional sign for Thompson's Peach and Pecan Orchards. Fifteen minutes later, Duncan took another right. A couple minutes later, the road ended in front of the covered porch of a two-story, whitewashed farmhouse. The front door opened, and a tall brown hair braided lady in a gray dress and white full apron came out and walked to the truck. "Welcome, Violet, my sweet sister and Lily, my beloved niece!" As the ladies got out, Ida hugged and kissed them.

"This is Duncan McDougal and this is Andrew Miller. They are helping us move and unload," Violet explained.

"First, we must feed these men! There is a barn in the back where you can unload any items not urgently needed. Cover everything with hay to disguise until all goes well. There is a bunk room on the top floor of the barn for you, Duncan," instructed Ida. "But please, everyone, come inside and have a good breakfast first."

She held Violet and Lily's hands as they walked to the house. "Come in and wash up. There is a bathroom on the first floor for the men. Ladies, take the one on the second floor between your bedrooms." Ida felt a pang when seeing them. Violet was obviously a worn-out woman, and the child needed so many different things to make her whole. Ida promised God she would do all in her power to help them. What frightened Ida the most was that gorgeous Scotsman, Duncan. He ignited feelings she had not felt in a long time, and she was shocked at her reaction to him. She needed to control herself.

Duncan thought Ida was a striking woman. He loved the sound of her voice. She stirred in him what he had felt for his wife, Eleanor, when they first met. Sadly, he had lost Eleanor years before. Since her death, he had been lonely. Helping Violet and Lily made him miss Eleanor even more, and now he was surprised by the beautiful, widowed Ida. He knew he'd better watch himself. This was Tom's sister.

Still, he was going to enjoy collaborating with her to help Violet and Lily.

The country kitchen was large. Ida took the food out of the warm oven. On the dining room table, she arranged platters of pancakes, eggs, bacon, and toast. Butter, syrup, and jams were placed there as well. Carefully, she took off the stove hot pots of coffee and tea. Lastly, she brought in cream and sugar containers along with a pitcher of cold milk for Lily. The men ate heartily then thanked Ida for a wonderful breakfast. They brought in two carpet bags and several boxes marked to go inside. The boxes were labeled as sheet music, legal papers, and sewing supplies. According to the Violet, the rest could wait. The sewing machine and piano were not yet needed inside, as Ida had both available. The men took the other belongings to the barn and covered them with hay.

The ladies thanked Andrew for all his help. They offered to pay him, but he would not except anything but Aunt Ida's strawberry jam. Duncan drove him to the train station to get back to Macon, then drove his truck back to Ida's and into the barn. Tomorrow, he would paint the signs to read "Ida's Produce." He was to help deliver her goods as one of his jobs. He would especially be on alert for

George. You never know what an unstable person will do, and he was glad he had the strength of a mover and the military skills from his days of service. Hopefully, he would not need them.

The ladies helped Ida clean up, then Ida directed them to sit in the living room to talk. There was a howling sound. Ida excused herself, opened the kitchen door to let the howler in, and the two walked back into the living room. "This is King, my bluetick hound." King went straight to Lily and licked her face clean. "Enough, King! Go eat your dinner." Off to the kitchen he went while the ladies laughed. "He has free reign around my property and makes sure unwanted animals and people are scared off. At the least, he loudly warns me. Sometimes, he thinks he is bringing me a present, but really, it's a dead mouse or rabbit." Everyone laughed. King came back and sat next to Lily.

"Lily, why don't you take King out back and throw a stick? He will bring it back to you over and over. He loves that game," instructed Ida. Lily got up, and King followed her outside.

There was a good deal Ida needed to know so she could help these damaged ladies. How much had they endured, and how had they coped? Could she be of any help to them, or did Violet feel she could not confide or get help from anyone? "Okay, Violet. Tell me everything so I can help. Do not leave anything out. I do not want any surprises to arise. I need to be prepared just in case. I understand your husband was verbally abusive, and we know how that typically grows then ends. In other words, lives are at risk."

Violet told her all, even everything dealing with George that she had never told Carolyn or Tom. She talked about how George verbally tortured Lily. How Carolyn and Tom showed Lily not everyone was like her father. Even with other family members' love and acts of kindness, Lily felt rejected and unloved by her father, which of course, caused a lot of emotional turmoil for Lily. She said, "I know I should have left years ago. I am ashamed that I didn't, but I guess I needed my breaking point. This last demand was my breaking point."

"Okay. Thank you for your honesty. We need not speak of this again."

Lily and King entered the room. King was panting. Ida gave instructions, "Violet, you take the purple room, unpack, and take a nice bath then a nap. These last several days have been exhausting for you. I will take care of Lily. Lily, you are to unpack in the room with teddy bears, boats, and horses. Pick out a change of clothes and meet me in my bathroom. I have a wonderful shampoo for your hair. First, we need to give King a bowl of water." So off they went as instructed.

Ida filled the bathtub with scented bath salts she had personally made. Lavender was relaxing and smelled wonderful. She also had lavender-scented bar soap and a bath sponge ready just for Lily. She let Lily bathe privately but said to knock on the wall when she wanted help shampooing her hair. Ida loved taking care of a child again. How she missed her son. She could not wait to share cooking, canning, and playing the piano. Lily knocked on the wall. Lily had already dunked her head in the water to get her hair wet, which made Ida laugh. Ida took the bottle and poured a small amount into one hand then rubbed it between both palms. Slowly, she spread the rich shampoo throughout Lily's hair then massaged it through long strands from her scalp. The aroma and affection were heavenly for little Lily. Not even her mother was this attentive. A moan escaped her lips, which surprised Ida. The child's expression said what her voice would not, "This is wonderful, Aunt Ida. I love the lavender scent and being in a warm, safe place. Thank you."

Ida responded to the unspoken words, "I am glad you are enjoying this. I am enjoying doing this for you. I wish I had a daughter to do and share things with. And now I have you, my sweet niece. I miss my husband and my son, but boys are a handful and get into so much trouble that dads tend to love them more for all their antics."

Lily knew this from her cousins Frank and Tom and grinned at recent memories. She was going to miss her weekly visits to her cousins, especially, the overnights with Savanah. She sighed. She would have King instead. He would have to do. It was not going to be so bad.

Ida said, "Now dunk into the water to get all the bubbles out of your hair. You're finished. I will let you dry yourself and dress in private. I will wait in my bedroom to brush out your hair."

When Lily came out, Ida walked Lily to a chair in front of a vanity. Lovingly, Ida took a brush and slowly brushed out any tangles, smoothing out Lily's hair. Then, she pulled the hair back into a ponytail at the base of her neck and tied a large white bow. Ida handed Lily her hand mirror to admire her work. The reflection made her eyes look large and beautiful. This was not the mousey brown-haired girl who just arrived.

Lily was shocked! Was this really her? She smelled and looked beautiful! Lily turned and kissed Ida's cheek then bear hugged her tightly in thanks.

"You're welcome, Lily. Smile more and be happy. No one will recognize you here. I promise. Could you please help me make dinner and set the table?"

Lily smiled and nodded yes.

The dinner table was set with platters of food. Ida said a prayer then dishes were passed around, and everyone started to eat. Ida asked what they would like to do to help. Violet decided to weed and take care of the vegetable garden, pick fruit when needed, help with washing and ironing, and help with cooking and cleaning in the kitchen. Duncan volunteered to take goods to the market on Saturdays and Tuesdays, repair anything needed, do any tasks and errands Ida wanted, and to help keep an eye on Lily. Ida explained to Lily that she would like her to help cleaning the house, canning and preserving vegetables, and overseeing King. Her main jobs were to bathe, brush, feed, and play with King. Everyone agreed that after breakfast on Sunday mornings, they would go to church. All would help prepare the meals. The rest of each day, after chores, was free time. Whatever else may arise, they would deal with it then. All agreed. Life was going to be wonderful. Violet looked at her smiling, safe daughter and sighed as loving relief washed over her spirit.

Chapter 4

Everything went remarkably smoothly for three months. One day, Duncan was out back putting up a swing for Lily, as Violet knew Lily missed swinging very much. Violet went to pick some vegetables for dinner. Ida and Lily were making lunch. King woke up from his nap on the kitchen floor by the back door and started to bark. His barking and walking all the way to the front door alerted Ida that someone was approaching. "Let us see who is here. Lily, stay behind me until I look through the keyhole. It might be your father." Lily nodded that she understood. Ida looked then felt relieved. "It is okay, King. Sit." King stopped barking and sat next to Ida. "Lily, it is a police officer. Just act like you are my niece, of course." Ida opened the door. "Good afternoon. How may I help you?"

"Sorry to bother you at lunchtime. I am Sargent Adams. A Mr. Rollan has requested our office to search for his missing wife, Susan Rollan." He handed her a terrible sketch. "Have you seen her?" Then he handed her another sketch, "and this is the daughter, Catherine Rollan."

“I am afraid I have not seen either one. They look so sad,” answered Ida.

“I know. Between us, after learning about Mr. Rollan, I hope I never find them, but I have a job to do. Thank you for your time. Have a good day.” He turned and left.

Ida and Lily went to the garden to talk with Violet. Violet saw them coming and stood up. “What’s up?”

“A police officer was here with horrible sketches of you two. Fortunately, he did not recognize Lily. I said I had not seen either person. He will not be back. But George may search here later, so in the coming months, we must be alert. Something told George to come here, so I’m worried he knows more than we think.” Ida explained.

“I agree. Better safe than sorry, but let’s be as normal as we can be,” replied Violet.

“God is watching over us. We will do an extra thank you to him tonight in our prayers,” said Ida.

Chapter 5

Nine months safely passed after the police officer's visit. Violet and Ida realized they missed Lily's birthday last year and decided to celebrate this time. Ida's family had always celebrated birthdays with the person's favorite meal and cake and something handmade. And of course, a loud singing of "Happy Birthday!"

They made meatloaf, mashed potatoes with gravy, and green beans. No cake for Lily. She wanted peach pie. After singing and dessert, Ida had everyone go into the living room. Violet and Ida had not allowed any piano playing in fear George might be snooping around, but it was time to put fears away and start afresh.

Everyone took a seat except Ida. She picked up a basket by the piano bench and handed it to Lily. "Happy tenth birthday," said Ida. The basket contained lavender handmade bath salts and bar soap, a bath sponge, and that wonderful shampoo.

Lily kissed and hugged Ida as a thank you.

Next, Duncan got up and handed her a decorative wooden box. "Happy birthday. At the bottom there is a key. Give it three turns, then lift the front lid."

Lily turned the key then lifted the lid and heard "The Blue Danube Waltz."

"It is beautiful!" She kissed and hugged him.

"Lily, did you just talk?" asked Duncan.

"I did." She looked as shocked as everyone else in the room. Violet was immediately in tears.

"Why now?" he asked.

"I feel safe, protected, and loved. You do special things for me."

"You are coming out of your shell, sweetie," exclaimed Ida.

Everyone hugged Lily with joy. Violet said, "My precious daughter, today is your birthday, but you have given us the real gift—a sign of healing in your heart. How wonderful it is to hear your sweet voice! I'm beside myself, but I must now give you my gift. I was going to make this last year but did not get a chance. I hope you love it," anxiously said Violet. She handed Lily a box, from which Lily unwrapped a beautiful pink calico dress with matching hat and a gorgeous white apron, along with an assortment of colored ribbons carefully tied in a large knot so they would not tangle.

"Oh, mother! These are beautiful! I must try them on now," gleefully said Lily.

She went quickly to her room and changed clothes, then ran down to show everyone. Her heart was so overjoyed that it was racing. “Thank you all for making this day so special,” cried Lily.

“Not over yet,” said Ida as she sat down on the piano bench at her baby grand piano. “I would like to play Mozart’s ‘Nine Variations in D.’” Fingers quickly flew over the keys. The music was lively and wonderful. Everyone clapped as Ida finished and stood up. She turned toward Lily.

“Lily, I would like for you to play something,” Ida requested.

Lily blushed but eagerly sat at the piano. This piano was much larger than her mother’s. She felt a little unsure of herself.

“It is the same keyboard with just a larger body. Relax,” encouraged Violet.

Lily took a deep breath before she lightly touched the keys and pedals. It was the same. She did relax, and she let the melody flow throw her mind to her fingers as she started to play “The Blue Danube Waltz,” just like the music box. How she missed playing. Her body was throwing all her will and love into the keys. She did not miss one note. Playing the piano always took her to a wonderful place no matter how soft or violent the music.

Something took over her soul and body. It was a joy she could never describe. The piano was her escape from her father. It was the love of her mother. It was her joy. When she finished, her mother, Ida, and Duncan were on their feet and clapping.

"Thank you for that wonderful performance. I know you have not played for a year, but you were excellent. This performance gave me an idea where you are and what needs to be worked on. I will instruct you on Sunday and Wednesday afternoons for three hours. You may practice whenever you have time. The piano is at your convenience. Just not when we all are sleeping or sick." Everyone laughed.

Today, Violet noticed how lovingly Duncan looked at Ida. She had noticed him admiring Ida more and more. Was he falling in love with her? She also noticed Ida admiring the handsome man. He would be perfect for her. *If I were not married, I would go after him*, thought Violet as she laughed to herself. *Time will tell, but maybe. I can speed things along.*

Chapter 6

Back in Macon, Georgia, George was steaming. *The witch has left me for that dumb girl and after all that I have done for her? Is she crazy!?* Then he found out that her mother left the deed to their house in her sister's name not Susan. The sales proceeds from the house were lost to him. He was left with only their meager savings account. Instead of purchasing a prideworthy home, he would have to rent an apartment. He thought, *That witch has really screwed me all the way around.* He asked her sister and brother-in-law where she was, but they said they had no idea. They even accused him of killing his own wife and daughter.

George had the police looking for Susan and Kitty, but to no avail. He could not get a divorce without finding her. He decided to tell everyone they died in a fire. He was going to find a moronic, needy young girl. If she produced for him a son, then he would marry her. Not before. He was no dummy. He wanted a better life than what he had, and now he could create just that. Life is hell, but after a few drinks, it always looks better.

Chapter 7

June 1889

Two more years passed without any problems for Violet and Lily. The foursome on the farm had a regular routine. The Harris family visited for holidays and special weekends. When they visited, Carolyn and Tom took Ida's bedroom. The boys took Lily's bedroom. Aunt Ida slept on one living room sofa, and Violet slept on the other. Savanah and Lily slept on the living room floor cocooned in quilts. Savanah and Lily loved the warmth from the fireplace during the cold and the smell of pine during Christmas. Uncle Tom built a second swing so the girls could swing together. Life was becoming normal.

Duncan made the boys slingshots and used bales of hay and tin cans for targets. Fishing was another fun sport for all, even though Savanah seemed to catch the most every time. King loved having the boys around. They would wrestle with him and swim in the pond way in the back when the weather was warm. Everyone accepted Duncan as part of the family. They still did not dare visit the Harris family in Macon.

Duncan was just outside the barn, getting the truck ready for tomorrow's drop-off with Ida's goods. King and Lily walked up and stopped to watch. "Hello, Lily and King," greeted Duncan.

"We are taking a walk before my birthday dinner," answered Lily. King lay down by the barn door.

"Can you keep a secret?" asked Duncan.

"Of course, I can! What is it?" replied Lily.

Duncan wiped his hands with a rag then placed it on the truck. He came around and stood in front of Lily. He reached into his pocket and pulled out a small wooden box then opened it to show Lily. There inside was a half-carat, round ruby surrounded by tiny diamonds in a gold setting. "I am going to ask Ida to marry me. Do you think she will like it?" asked Duncan.

Lily beamed, "She will love it. She loves red. It is beautiful. Now that you are going to marry Aunt Ida, do I get to call you Uncle Duncan?"

"Yes, you do, unless you don't want to," he asked.

"I would like that very much, Uncle Duncan," she hugged him.

"Let us see if she will accept. Maybe we can celebrate your birthday and our engagement tonight. Let me get cleaned up, and I will be right in."

"Come on King," Lily commanded. Off they walked for a while before returning to the house to wash for dinner.

Everyone was in the kitchen helping put platters of food on the table. Once done, Ida and Duncan were the only ones left in the kitchen. Duncan turned Ida around by the shoulders to face him. He dropped to one knee, then asked, "Ida, I loved you the minute I laid eyes on you. Would you do me the honor of marrying me?" he asked softly.

"Yes, Duncan. I will marry you. Over these two years, you have shown me what a wonderful person you are. How could I not fall in love with you?" she answered.

Duncan took the ring and placed it on her finger. "Oh, Duncan! It is breath taking!"

"I'm so glad you like it."

"How did you know I love red?"

"I already know a lot about you, but I hope to learn a lot more when we're married."

They entered the dining room beaming. “I’m engaged to Duncan!” Ida cried out as she showed everyone her ring.

Violet and Lily got up and hugged Ida and Duncan. “Congratulations!” they yelled.

“When is the big day?” inquired Violet.

“The sooner the better,” replied Duncan.

“Tomorrow, we will call on Reverend James to see what dates suit him,” quickly answered Ida.

They celebrated Lily’s twelfth birthday and the engagement. What a joyful day!

Ida and Duncan married two weeks later. The Harris family came up for the weekend ceremony and celebration, then stayed to help around the farm. Ida and Duncan honeymooned in Savanah, Georgia, for ten days. Duncan then revealed to Ida how wealthy he was. He did not care about the money and wanted a simple life. Ida agreed. With his wealth, they would help others whenever needed. Duncan and Ida learned more about each other and were thrilled to start their lives together.

Chapter 8

July 1891

Aunt Ida sat at the kitchen table with a hot cup of coffee. She contemplated Lily. She had progressed to where Ida couldn't do anything more. She thought about contacting her mentor, Lorenzo Tucci in New York. Lily's playing had advanced beyond Ida's expectations.

She needed to talk this over with Violet. She needed to be up front about everything she could so Violet could make a drastic decision if the opportunity arose. If Violet thought it would be good to go to New York with Sal and Lorenzo, Ida would write to Lorenzo to come.

Violet entered the kitchen. "Coffee smells great, and I cannot wait to have a cup."

Violet took her coffee and sat across from Ida.

"I have an idea I want to discuss with you. I first want you to listen to all I have to say, then give me your opinion now or think about it first."

"I am all ears," replied Violet.

Ida took a deep breath then continued," As you know, I was tutored by Lorenzo Tucci in New York for two years. I stayed with him and his partner, Sal.

They have a mansion so there were plenty of rooms which could accommodate, even when my parents visited. Lorenzo and Sal are wonderful gentlemen and treated me like their daughter or niece. I never had to fear them. They were very protective." Ida looked up for help in continuing, then looked back at Violet. "Lorenzo and Sal never married because they could not lawfully marry. I never was told or witnessed any behavior that was inappropriate. There were a few quick looks of adoration and hints from how they worked together, argued, and read each other's thoughts. It felt like they were a married couple. Society could ruin them and send them to prison. I know it's against the law and church, but when you see them together… how could God not love all his children? They are written in the Bible without him condemning them; why should we?"

Ida looked at her cup of cold coffee then looked back up. She had to give Violet time to digest all she said. "I met my husband the second year, fell in love, gave up my career, married, and moved here. Lorenzo, Sal, and I still communicate once a year. I have gone as far as I can with Lily. I feel she needs more if she wants a career. I would like to write and ask Lorenzo to come and counsel. He will probably want to take her as his pupil. So, would you be willing to move with her to New York to let Lorenzo mentor Lily? Could you be comfortable living with Lorenzo and Sal, given what I've told you? You may need to take a couple of days to decide."

"Ida, I value your opinions. The only type of men I am against are like my husband and worse. It may take some time to get used to them because I know about them, but it would no matter what. I think it best not to say anything to Lily until we know for sure he is coming and whether he wants to mentor her. I don't want her to be disappointed." responded Violet.

"I hoped you would say that. I will write to him tomorrow. Moving away from this farm with no kids around could be lonely for a child. Hopefully, she will make friends in New York," said Ida.

"At our former home, she did not have any church or neighbor friends. They shunned her because she did not speak. She was lucky to have the Harris family and sleepovers with Savanah. Her music is her reality and breath. She will be fine. Thank you for doing so much for us. You are our angel," replied Violet.

"It was an honor to help. We will see what happens. I am exhausted. See you in the morning," stated Ida.

Ida decided then to go ahead and write to Lorenzo Tucci. She described Lily's background, what she had accomplished, and what she thought Lily needed. She would appreciate it if he visited and critiqued Lily's performances. She mailed the letter and anticipated his response.

Ida thought about Lorenzo. He is such a unique person. He is always happy and ready to help anyone no matter what. He plays every instrument, has a beautiful tenor voice, and is rich beyond measure. Being six feet six inches tall, with broad shoulders above a muscular, medium frame, he was striking. He kept his black wavy hair to the shoulders but trimmed around the face to frame his stunning blue eyes, Roman nose, Cupid lips, and a deep rich voice. He could make any woman swoon or throw herself at him. Just thinking about him made Ida a little moist, which made her blush.

She had long ago hoped to start a relationship with Lorenzo, but women were of no interest to him. He and his partner, Salvador DeMarco (known as Sal), were in love. The two were also co-owners of a business and thriving entrepreneurs. Sal was the vice president of their company, managed investments, handled legal issues, and did whatever Lorenzo requested. Lorenzo was the president of the company, a talent scout, a mentor to select persons with talent, and a silent investor. His recent investment is the new Carnegie Hall. Because of all this, he had a penthouse on one floor and private music rooms on another floor that were walled off from the ten guest practice rooms. There was another floor with a large kitchen to prepare food for parties, along with a huge ballroom. Another floor held bedroom suites with their own bathrooms for guest stars and Lorenzo's staff. Ida had heard that the main concert hall was breathtaking and hoped to see it soon.

Lorenzo wanted a little girl after his sister died. He could not adopt, even with all his money, just because he was single. So, he poured all his soul into mentoring. Ida hoped her letter would pique his interest, but if not, she knew he loved her biscuits and preserves.

Sal reached a height of five feet, ten inches, had hair like Lorenzo's but brown, brown eyes, and a stocky, muscular frame. He was attractive but not in the same category as Lorenzo. He walked into Lorenzo's office without knocking and handed him the letter. “This one must be important. It is from Ida.”

Lorenzo took the letter opener and slit the top. He unfolded the letter and read. A smile crossed his face. *A prodigy!* “Sal, respond to Ida by wire. I want her to get my response quickly. We will be there next week, on Monday, at about 10:30 AM. Biscuits and preserves are necessary! Include that we only have a few hours to spare. Check the train schedules for late night or early morning, make a hotel reservation if necessary, and reserve a carriage for the morning.”

“Right away,” chimed Sal as he walked out the door. This was great news for Lorenzo, as he needed a new project. He had not found anything or anyone of interest or worth his time in the last couple of months. Sal could not wait for this trip.

Chapter 9

Ida received the response with excitement. They were celebrating Lily's fourteenth birthday. Ida decided to disclose her thrilling news during dinner. She told them about writing to her mentor, Lorenzo Tucci, about Lily. She explained that his partner, Salvador, would accompany him here on Monday at 10:30 AM. Lorenzo would listen to Lily then advise. Everyone was excited.

"Will he be my next teacher?" Lily sheepishly asked. She felt concerned. She was so happy and secure here.

"I hope so. He is a truly kind gentleman. His sister, Sophia, died two years ago of cancer. She was a professional violinist. He has not recovered from losing her. He tried to adopt a little girl because he misses Sophia so much and longs to be a father, but even with his fortune, as a single man, he is not allowed to adopt. He was a wonderful brother and father figure to Sophia. Sal even helped raise her like a big brother. All of you will adore these men. But I warn you ladies, Lorenzo is extremely attractive. He does not care to use it to his advantage."

Ida turned to Duncan then patted his chest, “My love, you are my extremely attractive Scotsman, though.”

Everyone laughed.

“Lily, what would you like to play for Lorenzo?” inquired Ida.

“Waldleufel’s ‘The Skaters’ Waltz.’ Is that okay?” suggested Lily.

“That would be excellent. I know you are a little nervous, you need not be. They will not bite. They are both sweet and funny. I recommend before you play, you go outside and twirl. Then stop, take a deep breath, and come back inside. Stand in front of the piano. Introduce yourself and what piece you will be playing. Sit down. Take another deep breath, then play your heart out. Once done, stand and smile. All will take its’ own course from there. You will be fabulous. Do not worry,” instructed Ida.

“Thank you, Aunt Ida, for taking excellent care of me. I love you.” They hugged.

“It is my pleasure, dear one. I love you, too,” responded Ida. She hoped all would go well. The future was now in God’s hands.

Chapter 10

The big day had finally arrived. Everyone was nervous and excited. Violet let Lily out back at 10:25 AM to twirl and relax. At exactly 10:30 AM, a knock on the door alerted everyone that Sal and Lorenzo had arrived. Duncan let Ida open the door and take control of the visit.

"Welcome, gentlemen," she hugged both men. "Please come in. This is my husband, Duncan." The men firmly shook hands.

"I have heard wonderful stories about you both. It is a pleasure to finally meet," expressed Duncan. "Let me take your coats and hats."

"Gentlemen, follow me into the living room to meet Lily's mother," directed Ida.

As they entered the room, Violet rose from her chair. Her mouth fell open from gawking at Lorenzo. She realized how horrible she must look and quickly closed her mouth. "I am Violet, Lily's mother. It is a pleasure to meet you. Thank you for taking time to listen to Lily. Please sit down. Do you want anything to drink or eat?" Violet offered.

They both replied no. The men sat on the sofa, but Lorenzo had to stretch out his long legs after the trip. He hoped they would not trip anyone.

In the meantime, Ida went to get Lily. Violet sat back on the chair. Then Ida and Duncan sat on the opposite sofa.

Lily finished twirling in her new pink dress with matching hair bow, took a deep breath, walked into the living room, and stood in front of the piano. She focused on the painting above the sofa so she would not be looking at the men. She relaxed a little more then began, "My name is Lily Mae Faye. I would like to play 'The Skaters' Waltz' for you." Ida's trick had worked. She felt confident as she sat on the piano bench then placed her fingers on the keys. Her mind visualized the notes, and her soul felt them. She began to play with great passion.

She finished, then stood in front of the piano and bowed as everyone rose to their feet to applaud. She finally looked at Sal. What a kind face. She looked at Lorenzo and was struck by his beautiful smile. His expression made her feel loved, cherished, and protected as a daughter might if she were lucky enough to have a kind father. She felt silly to feel that way, but still, she smiled back like a pleased daughter might.

Lorenzo watched as the cutest young girl entered the room. She was obviously shy, which he recognized when she focused on the painting instead of him. When she played, he was amazed at her talent. He could see how she felt the music as she played. But there was something else. He felt protective of her, he wanted to nurture her, he wanted to make her laugh and be happy. These were not like feelings for a wife. These were emotions he felt toward Sophia. Could she be a daughter for him? Would Violet object? After a minute of applauding, he walked up to her then went down on his knees so that they were eye to eye. "That was beautiful." He remembered after a concert his sister gave how proud he was—just like now. A tear rolled down his smiling face.

"Thank you. Why are you crying?" Lily took a finger and wiped the tear away.

"You overwhelmed me with your talent. You remind me of the beloved sister I lost two years ago." He smiled his best smile. "I would be honored to take you under my care and guide your career. You and your mother would live with us in the penthouse. All expenses paid. If it does not work out for you, I will bring you both back to Ida."

"It would be my honor," answered Lily. She put a hand on each of his cheeks. "You have the most beautiful smile."

Another tear ran down Lorenzo's cheek. He was remembering when Sophia and he were young. If he cried, she would take her fingertip and wipe the tears away, one by one. "I must confess when I first saw you, I strangely felt that you are the daughter I've been waiting for."

"I feel the same way about you. May I call you Papa?" she asked.

"Yes, my little bird," he joyfully replied. He turned toward Violet. "Violet, is it all right for Lily and me to be like father and daughter and you and me like sister and brother? I feel such a strong connection," asked Lorenzo as he held his breath for the reply.

"It seems God had this planned," answered Violet.

Lorenzo let out a sigh and got up. He hugged Lily and kissed her forehead.

"You only need to pack what you both want. Sal will pick you up on Friday," instructed Lorenzo.

"I have my mother's piano and a sewing machine with supplies. We only have a couple of boxes and one carpet bag each," explained Violet.

"You can put the piano and sewing machine in your suite. Lily will have a grand piano of her own to practice on. I promise, if you decide not to stay, I will bring you back to Ida." Violet nodded in understanding. Everyone started hugging. Ida then instructed them to be seated in the dining room for lunch and biscuits with preserves.

Ida was amazed at what had happened. What a surprise! This was better than she expected. Something profound had taken place between two creative, longing souls who shared a love of music.

Sal and Lorenzo said their goodbyes. Before leaving, Lorenzo went to Lily, rubbed her arm, and said, "Sing, Little Bird, sing. I may have just met you, child, but I love you."

Lily replied with a hug, "I love you, too, Papa." She felt so wonderful. Her own father had never said a kind word or kissed or hugged her. She felt wanted and loved. He nicknamed her Little Bird, but what did he mean by "Sing, Little Bird, sing?" She would find out later. She and her mother were soon off on another journey.

Chapter 11

The next morning, Lily came down for breakfast to find Violet and Duncan had already eaten and were busy outside.

"I will make you pancakes with lots of butter and syrup. Would you care for bacon?" asked Ida.

"Oh, yes please," answered Lily. "Is it really true what happened yesterday, or was it a dream?"

"True, my dear. The four of you are meant to be together. Sal told me he was so happy to have you both in the family," answered Ida.

"What did Lorenzo mean by, "Sing, Little Bird, sing?" asked Lily.

"Little bird is a baby bird. He cannot fly, find food, protect himself, or sing yet. When the bird learns to fly, catch food, and protect himself, he no longer chirps but has a song; he can fly away and be on his own. Lorenzo is encouraging you to develop your skills, be strong, and be independent so you can live on your own," explained Ida.

"That is wonderful. I like calling him Papa," exclaimed Lily.

"He loves it when you call him Papa. He beams with delight. He is true to his word. If you want to come back, he will safely bring you here. We would love for you to stay," assured Ida.

"I am glad my mother will be his sister. I wish it would become more," said Lily.

"I am afraid Lorenzo had enough of women and prefers it that way. He will never marry," responded Ida. This was a delicate subject, and Ida thought she managed it well.

"Too bad, but it is his choice," Lily said sadly.

Ida placed the food in front of Lily and said, "Now eat. Then find what you are going to take with you. Your mother will be in soon."

On Friday, Sal arrived with a moving truck. It took only a half-hour to load the truck. After the truck left for New York, Ida made everyone lunch. She hugged, kissed, and said her goodbyes to Violet and Lily and wished them a safe trip. Then Duncan lifted Lily into the back of the truck to sit; Violet and Sal sat in front with Duncan. Off they went to the train station. "This feels like déjà vu. I, once before, drove you ladies to someone to help you; now I am driving you to someone *new* to help you," Duncan said as he thought about their journey these past years.

"It feels so strange," Violet said with apprehension.

They arrived at the train station and thanked Duncan for everything he had done for them. They hugged and said their goodbyes. Once seated inside, they waved at Duncan as the train pulled away.

The ladies were excited. This was their first train ride and first visit to New York. Time flew by for the ladies due to Sal's tour guide banter. They were surprised that the usually reserved Sal eagerly shared all he knew about New York City. He gave the ladies an idea of what it is like to live there and what goes on in such a big city. He even surprised himself but wanted to make the ladies more comfortable and less anxious about New York. Violet would be his sister and Lily would be his niece, he decided. Life was going to be lively and so much fun.

They arrived in New York City and found Lorenzo and his driver, Ricardo, waiting on the platform. Lorenzo had a nosegay of violets for Violet and a lily of the valley nosegay for Lily. The ladies were touched. They hugged before Ricardo drove them to Carnegie Hall's back entrance. The entrance had a portico which led to the interior, large lobby with a counter on the back wall for the concierge and bellhop. There were two open cage fronts called "elevators" on the left wall and one on the right wall. The one to the right was Lorenzo's personal elevator. A key was needed to open the door. They went straight up to the top floor for the penthouse. This was another new experience for the ladies. They held onto a railing inside as their balance was unsteady. Lorenzo said they would eventually be able to keep their balance.

Once they reached the top floor, the elevator opened to a landing. Sal opened two wooden doors so they could enter the foyer of the penthouse. The room had tall ceilings, Italian furniture and décor, cream walls, a wooden floor, and beautiful molding. The wall décor added to the room more subtle colors. A large bronze crystal chandelier brightened the area. Scattered around side tables were red brocade chairs.

The butler, James (a tall, blue-eyed, brown-haired Englishman of medium weight), pleasantly greeted them. He took their hats and coats.

"James, please set up refreshments in the parlor for us while I take the ladies on a tour."

James nodded and left.

"This is an entrance to the penthouse. Sometimes, clients use this area as a waiting room for Sal or me. This is also where we greet friends and family. To the left is Sal's and my office with a large conference room. To the right is the library. You may read any book on the shelves. There are lovely chairs, tables, and a fireplace to warm the room in the winter. Opposite the entrance doors, the left door opens to a huge coat room. The right door opens to the ballroom, also called the festivities room." They entered the festivities room to see stunning French and Italian décor. Sofas, chairs, and side tables aligned the walls. Several card tables with chairs were scattered in the middle of the room. Some were square for four players, and others were larger, round tables for other games. A huge fireplace stood guard in the wall where they entered. Three large crystal chandeliers hung and brightened the room. Lorenzo continued, "The door on the right wall leads into the parlor. The parlor is a comfortable and small gathering room. On the left side, the door leads to the formal dining room. The kitchen is farther down on the right. Opposite the entrance wall, the door to the left of the leads to our personal dining room. The right door leads to our personal hall for our bedroom suites."

He led them through the left door to a well-appointed dining room which could seat up to twenty people with a long sideboard on the ballroom wall side. The opposite wall had two glass

French doors. “These French doors lead out onto a long, lovely terrace. You can explore later. The door on the left wall and to the left leads into the kitchen. The door to the right leads to four guest suites with their own bathrooms. Follow me so I can show you your rooms. Notice on the left of the hall, the center half has floor-to-ceiling windows to bring in the light and the terrace scene. The first suite is Sal’s,’ the second suite is mine, and Lily, this third one is your own suite.” He opened the door and let her enter first. “I hope you like it. You have a bedroom, sitting room, and bathroom with a walk-in clothes closet.” The suite was decorated in pinks and greens with white trim. A full-size, white canopy bed was adorned with a pink ruffled bedspread and matching canopy top. White throw pillows leaned along the headboard. A white writing desk and chair sat in front of the sitting room’s large window. The room included a pink velvet, chaise lounge chair, a white side table and coffee table, and a reading lamp. Paintings of flowers and dogs decorated the walls. Lorenzo and Sal held their breath in hopes she loved it.

“Oh Papa! My room is beautiful,” cried Lily. She hugged both men. “I feel like a princess.”

They were so thrilled she loved the room. They could breathe again. “I am so glad you like your room,” proudly said Sal. “It is getting late, and I still have work that needs my attention before I go to bed. I will see you both tomorrow for breakfast.” Lorenzo nodded in thanks and said goodnight to Sal.

“Thank you for everything and goodnight,” said both ladies in unison.

“Now, let’s go to the end of the hall, Little Bird, and show Violet her room,” added Lorenzo.

He opened the door to a room decorated with purple and green with white trim. Like Lily’s room, white furniture was spread around the bedroom. The full-size bed was accented with a quilt of purple, green, and white. Purple, green, and white throw pillows were arranged across the headboard. The sitting room held a purple velvet chaise lounge chair and the same tables and lamp. Paintings of flowers and country scenes decorated the walls. As the sitting room was larger, Violet could picture where she could place her piano and sewing machine. “This is beautiful. I do not feel worthy,” exclaimed Violet. Lorenzo hugged her shoulders and said, “Yes, my dear sister. You deserve all of this and much more.” He kissed her forehead and let her go.

"I will let both of you freshen up. Then, meet me in the parlor for our refreshments before both of you crash. Do you remember how to get there?"

"Yes," replied Violet. "The floor plan is simple."

Lorenzo was thrilled to know that they loved their rooms. Sal and Lorenzo would move the moon and stars for these ladies. Lily filled them with joy and love, and they hoped they did the same for her.

Finger sandwiches, sliced vegetable and fruit, an antipasto platter, a tray of cookies, and cannoli (along with pictures of iced tea and lemonade) were set up for them. The light dinner was welcomed. After twenty minutes, Lily's eyes started closing. Lorenzo lifted her up and carried her to her bedroom where Violet got her ready for bed. Lily tucked herself under the covers. Lorenzo came in and kissed her forehead and said, "Welcome home. Sing, Little Bird, sing. I love you."

"I love you, too Papa," Lily whispered in her sleep. She was out for the night. There would be only happy dreams that night.

Chapter 12

The next morning, the ladies washed, dressed, and went together to the family dining room. Chef Mario (a short, robust man with a cheerful disposition) awaited their arrival. In his Italian accent, he said, "Good morning. My name is Mario. I will be cooking for you. Sorry, Sal and Lorenzo had breakfast earlier. They wanted you ladies to sleep in after yesterday's long day. What beverages may I bring you?"

"I am Violet. It is a pleasure to meet you. I would like hot tea with lemon, please," answered Violet.

"I am Lily. It is nice to meet you. I would like a glass of milk please," answered Lily.

"I am preparing a special breakfast for your first day. I will be back in only a moment," Mario said with merriment and left.

A minute later, a server named Adele (a middle-aged black woman with deep brown eyes, short curly black hair, rounded figure, and a big smile) served their beverages.

They introduced themselves and found Adele very pleasant. Ten minutes later, she served them crepes filled with citrus ricotta cheese and topped with sauteed berries and whipping cream. It was so delicious the ladies moaned with every bite. Mario came in to see if everything was all right and if they needed anything else.

"Mario, your cooking is heavenly! We are going to get big and fat from eating your delicious food," complimented Violet.

Mario loved compliments. They reassured him that his passion for cooking was worthy, and that warmed his heart.

The ladies requested a lighter lunch as they could only imagine what he would be making for dinner. They suggested leftovers, which he laughed at. "Leftovers always go to the orphanage. No waste. They enjoy the food. And I can create more!"

They left to explore the penthouse and came across two maids in the festivities room. Both were named Mary. Mary Jane reached five feet two inches, had long brown hair and brown eyes, and was very thin. Mary Beth reached only five feet, wore a short brown hairstyle, also had brown eyes, and was a bit chunky. Violet asked for directions to the practice rooms. The Marys said Lorenzo would show them once he finished his meeting. The ladies moved on and entered the kitchen. While cooking, Mario was singing in Italian. He stopped and gave them a tour of his domain with pride and joy. The kitchen was large, well organized, and spotless. He showed them the special refrigerator just for them. They could get a beverage, water, or food for snacking anytime. There was a special cookie jar that was always full, but you never knew what cookie filled the jar. If they needed anything, they just needed to ask, and he would make it. If he was not in the kitchen, they just needed to dial "1" on the kitchen phone and tell him what they needed. He would be right up to make it. They thanked him for the tour, and Lily took a cookie with a smile.

They went out onto the terrace. The container gardens held vegetables and herbs to the left and right. Trees, azaleas, and roses aligned the sides of the terrace. The center had white, wrought-iron tables and chairs to allow for multiple seatings. It was heavenly.

Here is where Lorenzo found them. He was proud he could share what he had obtained with them.

"Lorenzo, this is breathtaking. The food was fabulous. I feel like I am in a dream and never want to wake up," explained Violet.

"May we see the practice rooms?" impatiently asked Lily.

"Of course, Little Bird. Ladies, follow me." They followed him to the elevator. He handed each a bracelet with a key. "This is your elevator key to use. But I request, when you plan to leave the building, I must assign a guard to escort you. This is for your safety," explained Lorenzo.

Violet understood. George was still out there. "Of course. We will let you or Sal know."

They entered the elevator as Lorenzo pushed a button labeled 5. "To go to my practice rooms, push number five for the fifth floor. My private rooms are separate from the six guest practice rooms, which use the regular elevators." He hoped they loved the rooms as much as he did. Music, helping people, and family were his passions.

They walked out, and he led them into the first room on the right side of the hall. "This is my instrument room. Sal arranged every kind of orchestra instrument to be in this room. If you are interested in learning to play any of them, let me know, I can teach you. I play all instruments," he said with pride.

"So many!" Lily was surprised. He became her idol. Someone to have so much knowledge and talent was extraordinary.

“The harp looks remarkably interesting. Maybe after I perfect the piano,” Lily responded.

They walked back into the hallway, and he pointed to two practice rooms on the left. Once they reached the end of the hall, he opened the door to a large room with two grand pianos facing each other and ten chairs in a row along the right wall. “This is my special room. What do you ladies think?” he inquired.

“It is wonderful,” responded Violet.

Lily went to the first piano. This was the first time she had seen such a large piano. She gently lifted the lid then lightly caressed the keys without playing. “No words can describe how I feel,” Lily responded dreamily, “I am just in awe.”

“The chairs are comfortable. Violet, you can sit, watch, and listen while Lily plays. We will start practice tomorrow. I want you to get to know your new home and feel comfortable living here. Let us go up and have lunch. I am hungry,” stated Lorenzo as he gently let down the lid of the piano. He was pleased with Lily’s reactions.

As they went up the elevator, Lorenzo continued, “Later today, I have a seamstress coming here to measure you both for a full wardrobe,” Lorenzo instructed.

"But we have very little money, and I can sew what clothes we need," cried Violet.

"We are family, Violet. I will always love and take care of you both," assured Lorenzo. "Violet, I have already thought about you. I realize you need something to do besides listening to Lily practice. I donate to a wonderful orphanage and have talked with the headmistress. She would love for you to come there tomorrow for tea and discuss what needs they have and see how you can help them. Ricardo will drive and escort you."

"What a wonderful idea! I would love to meet her. I know my sewing will come in handy. I will enjoy being busy and doing volunteer work. Thank you for your consideration, Lorenzo," said an appreciative Violet.

"We are family now. What is a family for!" requested Lorenzo.

Life had changed for Violet and Lily in ways they never could have imagined. Every morning and before bed, Lorenzo would rub Lily's arm and say, "Sing, Little Bird, sing. I love you."

And Lily would reply, "I love you, too, Papa."

He and Violet would hug good morning, hello, goodbye, and goodnight and say they loved each other as well.

Sal was the quiet and observant type. He let Lorenzo shine with pride. Like Lorenzo, he wished for a son to play with. He loved sports but did not have much free time. There were free times when Sal would go with one of the security guards to attend a boxing match, softball, basketball, or football game. Everyone found contentment in this newly formed family. Life was wonderful!

Chapter 13

Over the next two months, the family established a routine and took time to sightsee, dine out, and attend concerts, operas, and ballets at Carnegie Hall. Lorenzo worked with Lily on technique and some tricks of the trade. She was ready for the three pieces he chose for her. First would be Bach's "Air on the G String," followed by Chopin's "Mysterious Forest," with a finale of Claude Debussy's "Clair de Lune." She was learning at a fast pace, but he did not want to rush her. Lorenzo felt Lily needed four more months to be ready for her first public performance. He decided Valentine's Day would be perfect. All was set.

December 1891

Three months later was the beginning of December. The family sat at the breakfast table and discussed what was needed to make the penthouse ready for Christmas and for all their guests from Georgia. Shopping for a tree, decorations, and presents for the staff and family needed to be bought and brought home. They would hire horse drawn carriages for a ride around town which was the new rave. The kids would love ice skating, making snowmen, and having snowball fights. They would play games, cards, and sing Christmas songs. It was going to be a fun time. Lorenzo reminded the ladies that he would give Adele, Jasper, and the Marys time off Christmas Eve and Christmas Day to be with their families. Beds would not be made, and the family and staff would help Mario in cooking, setting the table, and clearing the table. Ricardo and James would help wash dishes. Sal and Lorenzo felt the staff was part of their family. They would join in the activities and everyone would dine together. In no time, they had the penthouse looking very festive and presents were stacked under the tree.

The ladies requested a personal shopping day. They secretly wanted to pick up something special for Sal and Lorenzo. Ricardo was to drive, escort, and eat lunch with them. They found a lovely cashmere red scarf, red hat, red leather gloves, and red socks for the flashy Lorenzo. For Sal, they bought the same items but in a conservative royal blue. The shop wrapped everything and added bows and tags. Ricardo put the packages in the car and asked the ladies what they would like for lunch. They heard about how wonderful Chinese food was and requested that. "I will take you to The Dragon's Den."

Ricardo was happy to suggest places. Mr. Cho Lin's restaurant was excellent. Just across the street, they entered the restaurant. Mr. Cho Lin greeted them like royals and seated them in the back corner. The place was decorated elegantly with lanterns, Asian murals, wooden figurines, and colors in red, gold, and white around black furniture. The white tablecloths and napkins gave a nice touch. The place was small—about twenty square tables for four. They ordered egg drop soup and egg rolls with duck sauce. Ricardo ordered Peking duck, Violet ordered egg foo young, and Lily ordered Szechuan shrimp.

Every bite was excellent. As they ate, the ladies asked Ricardo to talk about himself. He was easygoing and eager to share. They learned he was from the same town as Sal and Lorenzo, Lucca, Italy. Sal was his uncle. He was single with no girlfriend. He asked the ladies if everything was all right for them.

They said yes. They told him that life was like a fairy tale that they hoped would never end. Once they finished, Mr. Cho Lin brought hot jasmine tea and his famous almond cookies, which he personally baked fresh every day. They thanked Mr.

Cho Lin for such an excellent meal and headed home. Ricardo helped bring in the gifts and hid them in Violet's closet. The ladies thanked him for all his help. As he was leaving, he responded, "Any time. It was my pleasure." Exhausted, the ladies took a wonderful nap.

The past several months, to help the orphanage, Violet had been busy sewing together pants and shirts for the boys, dresses with matching hair bows for the girls, and coats for boys and girls. The Marys wanted to help, so they knitted scarves with matching hats and gloves for all. The ladies were using the formal dining room table to assemble their items into packages with each child's name on a tag to make sure each item was the right size and ready for the right person. They used the scarves as bows and placed a delicious candy cane in the center for a special treat. They were immensely proud of their work and hoped the packages of warm clothing would bring joy to each child.

Chapter 14

Time flew by, and guests were about to arrive. Lorenzo sent everyone two-way train tickets. He set up drivers to pick them up at the train station. Mario had a delicious spread of food laid out for everyone once they unpacked and freshened up. It was 1:45 PM when people started to arrive. Ida and Duncan were the first to be there. Once they were greeted, Violet showed them to the first guest suite. Fifteen minutes later, the Harris family arrived. Violet showed Carolyn and Tom the end, large suite.

"This place is unbelievable. Look at this room Tom. It is gorgeous! And you have an Italian cooking all your meals! I am never leaving," said the stunned Carolyn to Violet as she fell back onto the huge bed.

Sal showed the boys their room. The boys carried in their carpet bags and placed them next to a dresser. There were two full size beds. Each boy jumped onto a bed. "This is all just for us! Whoopie!"

"Glad you like it," laughed Sal. The boys jumped up and down on the beds, and Sal did not reprimand them. They kept up the antics until Sal took one of the pillows and started a pillow fight. After ten minutes, Sal stopped and said, "I would like to continue this, but unfortunately, I have work to finish before dinner. Love you boys. See you later," said Sal.

"Uncle Sal is so much fun," exclaimed Frank.

"That he is," replied Tom, Jr., as he wrestled Frank to the ground. The train ride had been a blast. This trip was not going to be so bad, thought the boys.

Lily and Lorenzo escorted Savanah to her room. "The next room is yours Savanah," said Lorenzo.

Savanah was not having any of it. She stomped her left foot and said, indignantly "I want to sleep with Lily! We are cousins, you know!"

"Sorry, Miss Savanah. No one told me," replied Lorenzo. "Let's get permission from your mother first."

They walked into Carolyn's room and explained.

"I am sorry Lorenzo. I should have known and told you. It is okay for them to sleep together. They always do, but I thought Savanah would like a spacious room of her own."

"Problem solved," said Lorenzo as the girls ran out of the room in the direction of Lily's room. He loved little girls. He never knew what they would say or do. He carried Savanah's carpet bag to Lily's room thinking this would be the family's first Christmas together. He wanted it to be perfect for them.

The girls entered Lily's room. Savanah was stunned by its beauty. "That is one big bed! This is like a princess room." They jumped on the bed for a minute then lay down side by side. "I am so happy for Aunt Violet and you. You are finally happy," whispered Savanah.

"I am," said Lily.

After a light meal, everyone went into the festivities room, and they were again in awe of the huge Christmas tree, decorations, and presents. The children played games while the adults played cards until dinner time. Mario, as usual, outdid himself. He presented veal scaloppini with delicate noodles, garlicky green beans, and slices of Italian bread smeared with a garlicky herb spread the boys loved. For dessert, he served lemon gelato with a curled sugar cookie.

"Mario, I am going home like a stuffed turkey. Your food is fabulous!" exclaimed Carolyn.

"You can stay with us and cook whenever you want," pleaded Ida.

Mario felt overjoyed and proud.

They all went back to the festivities room where Ida played the piano, and everyone sang Christmas songs. As she played Johann Strauss' "Emperor Waltz," James served eggnog as a nightcap.

"Thank you, Lorenzo," said Violet as she hugged him and kissed him goodnight.

"We are a family, and I love having a family," he sadly said as though in reflective thought.

She would later ask Sal about his past life. She somehow knew there was an incredibly sad story to be told.

Lorenzo picked up one girl in each arm after Savanah said goodnight to her parents. He was strong, tall, and could manage them. He brought them to their room. He dumped them onto the bed, leaned over to kiss Savanah's forehead, then kissed Lily's. As usual, he took Lily's arm and rubbed it while he said, "Sing, Little Bird, sing. I love you."

"I love you, too, Papa."

"Do not stay up too late. I will have James bring in a cart with drinks and snacks for you lovely ladies," added Lorenzo.

"That is a brilliant idea, Uncle Lorenzo. You are so thoughtful. Thank you," exclaimed Savanah.

"Thank you, Papa," said Lily.

“It’s my pleasure,” said Lorenzo. He knew they would be up late talking and need to sleep in late in the morning. He admired how girls bonded, fought, disagreed, but always came back together as if nothing happened to still be best friends.

In the meantime, Sal conversed with the boys, wrestled each, and sometimes both at one time with a finale of a pillow fight. He hugged each then said, “I will send James in with a cart of night snacks and beverages. Do not stay up too late. We have so much to do tomorrow. I love you. Goodnight,” said Sal. The boys immediately loved Uncle Sal and were glad he spent time with them. Sal enjoyed having the boys in his home, even though they wore him out.

Chapter 15

Christmas Eve went fast with brunch. Ricardo, Duncan, Tom, and Sal took the kids skating, helped them make snowmen, and hosted a snowball fight. The ladies went shopping then met the men for tea and hot chocolate and pastries at Mama Rosa's Bakery and Café. They came home to clean up and dress, then played games in the festivities room. Lorenzo assigned everyone to help Mario with the table. Once all were seated at the dinner table, Lorenzo said a blessing to start dinner. Guests were treated to an Italian "Seven Fishes with Pasta" dinner. No one had ever tasted calamari before. They loved it in the spaghetti sauce and stuffed with breadcrumbs and seafood. Dinner ended with a fruit cake called panettone, fresh fruit, nugget candy, and nuts. They loved it! Ricardo, James, Duncan, and Tom helped wash and dry the dishes, which took only twenty minutes. Mario said he would put all the dishes away later, and he thanked the men for all their help.

They gathered in the festivities room for more singing and games. James passed hot apple cider around before all went to bed. Everyone went to sleep right away. Lorenzo said his normal goodnight to Little Bird even though the girls were fast asleep. Sal was relieved the boys were fast asleep so he could go straight to bed. What a day!

Christmas morning arrived. Mario, James, Sal, and Lorenzo were the early birds. The men helped Mario set up the serving table with pancakes, scrambled eggs, bacon, Italian ham, sliced panettone, toast, fresh berries, butter, syrup, preserves, milk, coffee, hot tea, and hot chocolate. Whenever family members woke up, they could help themselves. Who woke up first? The boys, of course! Sal and Lorenzo hugged them good morning and wished them a Merry Christmas. They assisted the boys in their selection of food. The boys piled high everything on their plates and brought their select beverages to the table. Then the men filled their own plates. They talked while eating. Jokes and sports were big topics.

Ida and Duncan slowly joined them. Next, Carolyn, Tom, and Violet arrived. Finally, Savanah and Lily entered the room. When the girls were almost finished eating, there was a loud pounding, then a boisterous "HO! HO! HO!" came from the festivities room. Everyone was here. Who could that be, wondered the children. Quickly, the children got up and ran to the room. Santa was unpacking presents under the tree. “Merry Christmas everyone!” yelled Santa. James moved a wing chair next to the tree for Santa to sit down. “I know everyone has been good.” The men laughed. The boys snickered.

Violet ran to her room to get Lorenzo and Sal’s presents. With Ricardo’s help, she placed the presents with the other gifts then sat down.

Santa called Tom, Jr., to come and sit on his lap. Tom, Jr., was not having any of it, so James put a chair next to Santa for the boys. Santa handed him one present at a time to open. Tom, Jr., received gifts he could not have imagined and loved each one. He then opened gifts from family members. Next was Frank. When it was Savanah turn, she sat on Santa’s lap then pulled his beard and found it was real! She told him she was sorry for doubting.

Lily opened her packages. She did not ask for or want anything. She had all she wanted, but Santa gave her things she loved. Ida and Duncan gave her a knitted scarf and matching hat. Carolyn and Tom gave her a winter sweater. Then, Sal and Lorenzo carried a large box and placed it in front of Lily. They lifted the lid and let Lily look inside. Inside was the cutest golden retriever puppy. She lifted the puppy out of the box. “She is adorable. Sorry Santa and everyone, but this is my favorite gift!”

Violet asked, “What will you name her?”

“I’m not sure,” answered Lily.

“I have placed a food bowl, water bowl, and bed in the corner of the kitchen. There is a canister filled with dog biscuits,” instructed Mario, obviously proud of his added touches for the new pup.

“Thank you, Mario, for your thoughtfulness,” Lily said with gratitude.

“There are gifts for the adults, but I need to leave. I still have places to be,” exclaimed Santa. Lorenzo walked Santa to the elevator.

“Thank you for coming. You made their day. Did you have enough money for everything for the orphanage?” asked Lorenzo.

“More than enough. God bless you.”

Lorenzo handed him two envelopes. “This envelope is for you. It is my gratitude for all you have done for me. The other envelop, you may divide among your elf helpers. Merry Christmas,” said Lorenzo gratefully.

When Lorenzo returned, the staff and adults finished opening their gifts and thanked him for doing “too much.”

What is money for, thought Lorenzo.

Violet had Lorenzo sit in the chair by the tree and handed him the gifts she and Lily had chosen for him. He loved the red assortment and put everything on. Next, Ida and Duncan gave him a basket of preserves, and Ida promised to make biscuits before she left. Carolyn embroidered his initials on seven handkerchiefs as a gift from the Harris family. They were gifts of thought and made especially for him. Lorenzo was overwhelmed to receive such personal gifts. Sal received the same presents. He felt special as well.

Lorenzo handed Violet a box from Sal and himself. A beautiful gold bracelet with violets all around was engraved inside with, "Merry Christmas, 12-25-91, love Sal and Lorenzo." She cried as she hugged them.

Sal handed Lily a box. Inside was a silver chain with a filagree of lily of the valley. "Thank you both," cried Lily as she hugged them. Everyone helped clean up the room while Ricardo took the dog for a walk.

Ricardo and Sal took the kids for more ice skating and snow activities while everyone else helped Mario in the kitchen or set the table. Once the kids were back, the kids washed up and dressed for Christmas dinner. The adults helped place prime rib, roasted potatoes, roasted leg of lamb, roasted chicken, polenta, buttery rolls, glazed carrots, fresh fruit, and asparagus on the table. All sat down, then Lorenzo said the blessing. "The boys can really pack it away," said Lorenzo.

"They're growing boys," noticed Sal.

Everyone cleared the table for dessert. Mario served assorted cookies, a delicious custard, and cannoli. Everyone helped clear the table. The men washed the dishes. All met in the festivities room.

"I have a surprise for everyone. I have hired four horse-drawn carriages to drive us around as a special event," said Lorenzo. "Sal, Duncan, and the boys take the first one. Tom, Carolyn, and Ida, take the second. James, Mario, and Ricardo take the third carriage. Girls, you get to ride with Violet and me."

The girls yelled, "Whoopie!"

They had a wonderful time, but all were a little chilled even from under the heavy wool blankets. After the carriage rides, James served warm brandy and sherries to the adults. He served hot cocoa to the children. They drank by the large fireplace and warmed up quickly. All said goodnight. Half an hour later, Lorenzo went to say goodnight to the girls. Snuggled under the covers, the girls were ready to fall asleep. “Did you girls have a good time?”

“"This was the best Christmas ever, Uncle Lorenzo! Thank you so much," Savanah exclaimed as she hugged and kissed his cheek.

“The best Papa! Thank you. I have named my dog Sonata. What do you think?”

“It is perfect,” answered Lorenzo.

“It is perfect for you, Lily. I would have chosen Pecan because I just love pecans,” said Savanah.

They all laughed.

“Where will Sonata sleep?” asked Lily.

“In the kitchen. Mario has everything set for Sonata. She will be all snuggled and warm in her bed.” Lorenzo kissed both on the forehead then rubbed Lily’s arm saying, “Sing, Little Bird, sing. I love you.”

“I love you, too, Papa.”

“Goodnight and sweet dreams.” He closed the door.

“Did you boys have a good time?” asked Sal.

“The best!” both boys answered in unison.

“We love our train set and can’t wait to get it set up at home,” said Frank with a nod from Tom.

“Goodnight, Uncle Sal. Thanks for everything,” the boys told Sal.

“Goodnight,” said Sal as he hugged each one. He was going to miss them, and they were going to miss him.

All went well. Life was good at the Tucci home.

Chapter 16

January 1892

Two weeks later, all was back to normal. The tree and decorations were gone. Sonata was proving to be an obedient and routine dog. She went for a walk at 7:00 AM, 3:00 PM, and 8:00 PM.

Lorenzo decided to add another member to the staff. Jasper, Adele's sixteen-year-old son, would be in charge of Sonata. He would arrive and leave with Adele and eat meals with the family. He was known to have a unique way with animals. He worked with Sonata and Lily on commands and rewards. Adele appreciated Lorenzo hiring her son. It got him off the streets and away from his trouble-making friends. Jasper easily befriended the security staff of Patrick, Jackson, and Moses. Sometimes, the men would invite him to the sports events of which Adele approved.

Lorenzo waited for everyone to leave the breakfast table except Lily, Violet, and Sal. He cleared his throat then announced, "Lily and Violet, I would love to adopt Lily as my daughter and Violet as my sister. We love both of you and feel we make a great family. What do you think?"

Sal and Lorenzo nervously awaited the mother and daughter's responses. They hoped the ladies felt the same way they did.

Lily jumped out of chair and hugged Lorenzo, "Nothing would make me happier than to be your daughter, if it is okay with my mother."

Violet thought a minute then replied, "It would be okay with me, but she still has a legal father."

Sal rose from his chair and intervened, "Wonderful! I have papers that will cover every issue and make it all legal. I will discuss all and answer any questions in my office. If you ladies will follow me."

Sal's office was stunning. Wood paneled walls created a cozy environment. Two walls covered in bookshelves were filled top to bottom with books. A six-foot-long mahogany desk had files filling a stacker on the left, a couple of files in the center, and a container that held pencils, scissors, paper clips, and a letter opener to the right. At the front center edge was Sal's ink pen and ink well. A wooden trash can was half full of disposed papers that gave the room a lived-in look. Sal sat in his brown leather chair and directed them to take the two brown leather wingback chairs across from the desk. They waited for Sal to continue.

"Ladies, you do not know how happy we are that you both came into our lives. Lorenzo and I go back since childhood in Lucca, Italy. His family was extremely rich and lived in the Tucci Castle. Many were jealous and wanted them all dead. Mr. Tucci was not deterred from helping the poor and overseeing other needs. His father knew of plots to kill his family. This caused him to send his sister Sophia and Lorenzo to my family a couple of days before they were to take a ship to America."

He continued, "My father was a furniture maker and a good friend to Lorenzo's father. His father was smart and entrusted my father with their tickets and money. Lorenzo's infant brother, Jovani, stayed with his mother as he was still nursing. The night before they were to sail, his family was murdered, the castle ransacked and burned. Luckily, their money, jewels, and special items had been sent to banks and people they trusted in America months before. Because I was friends with Lorenzo, my father decided to use one of the tickets for me to go with them. We hid Sophia and Lorenzo until my Uncle Rocco came with his coach. We hid in the coach until we arrived safely at the dock. Lorenzo and I were only fourteen years old and Sophia only ten. In America, the Gambini family welcomed us at the dock and into their home. Lorenzo's father provided them with funds for a lifetime to take care of us. They did not care about the money; they wanted to help any family member in any way they could."

Sal took a calming breath as he looked to the heavens before he continued, "We attended college then did apprentice work in a law firm. Once we had a good background and decided what we wanted to do, Lorenzo took some funds, and we started our business, which, thankfully, broadened and grew. I am the vice president of the company and care for most of the financial and legal aspects. Lorenzo is the president, talent scout, fundraiser, and financial donator. By the way, he will not allow recognition for his generous contributions. This Carnegie Hall is one of his projects, which is why he has this penthouse and the practice rooms here. He loves to help prodigies. His sister was one of them. Unfortunately, she died of cancer. Lorenzo was so devasted, he would not come out of his bedroom for three months until I found a talent for him. He just finished helping him three months ago and was ready for another student. Luckily, Lily, we found you. You have given him a reason to live and so much more. We love you both. I will not say any more on this unless you have any questions."

They both shook their heads no.

"Lorenzo had a private detective follow George. He said that your husband is a piece of work. He used words I will not repeat. He is a drunk, which helped us. One night, he was so drunk, our detective offered him $100,000.00 if he would sign a document to promise he would never tell where the money came from and another document to state he received the funds. While he was signing, the detective put sleeping medication in his drink. By the time the bartender and waiter signed the papers as witnesses, he was out like a baby. I am sure he had the worst headache ever. While George was out, the detective put the money back in his case and left.

"This first document gives you, Susan, now known as Violet, of course, an uncontested divorce with no spousal demands, which means funds. You have legal rights to remarry if you wish. Please sign.

"In the second document, George gives up his rights to you, Catherine, now known as Lily. Lily, he has no hold on you, so Lorenzo has legal rights to adopt you as his daughter. These papers are for both of you to sign. Violet, you will legally be Lorenzo's sister, taking the permanent legal name of Violet Anne Tucci. Lily, you will legally be Lorenzo's daughter and known as Lily Mae Tucci. Please, both of you sign. Do either of you have any corrections or questions?" asked Sal.

"No," was their response.

"Not done yet. These papers pertain to his will. As his sister, you will receive $500,000.00 upon his death. Lily, you will inherit his estate minus funding for his projects and charities. Please sign. I will be both your advisor and the executor of the estate unless I am deceased, otherwise advised, or I appoint someone else. This is just to inform you. I will go over everything more fully when needed. Any questions?" asked Sal.

"Why us?" asked a still stunned but honored Violet.

"Because God put us together to be a family. Because in our odd circumstances, we needed each other to heal and finally be happy. I will enter these papers in court tomorrow and all should be settled. I will confirm at dinner tomorrow." Sal turned to Lily, "Lily, I would love for you to call me Uncle Sal." He got up and hugged her.

"Thank you, Uncle Sal. I love you, too." She kissed his cheek.

In a daze, Violet and Lily walked back to their rooms then fell fast asleep with a new kind of peace.

The next night, Mario made a delicious dinner of spaghetti and meatballs, garlic bread, and a salad. The desert was everyone's favorite, cannoli. Sal stood up and smiled, "The court accepted and finalized all the paperwork. Violet and Lily are legally Tucci's." Everyone hugged.

Chapter 17

February 1892

For the next two weeks, Lorenzo and Lily practiced on stage. He placed a glass of water on a small table next to the grand piano in case Lily became thirsty. Lily thought the music sounded amazing in the concert hall. She fine-tuned each piece and felt ready for the concert. Lorenzo had no advice to give. She *was* ready.

Everyone from Georgia arrived the day before the concert. They knew the drill when arriving. Of course, Savanah slept with Lily. The day of the concert, Mario served high tea before the concert. Later, a party would have various kinds of food and beverages.

Lorenzo gave James a box full of opera glasses. Each person would be able to see Lily closely. Lorenzo had the second booth to the right of the stage. There were no obstacles. One could see the full stage. Sal would escort Violet, Ida, Duncan, and Ricardo to the booth. James would escort the Harris family to the booth. Mario would bring a cart of beverages. The children, Violet, Carolyn, and Ida sat in the front row. Tom, Duncan, Sal, Ricardo,

James, and Mario sat in the second row. James passed out the glasses. Everyone was excited.

Lorenzo stood with Lily on the left side of the stage. He was dressed in navy evening attire. Lily wore a long black evening dress with a large black hair bow in her ponytail. Lorenzo peeked through the curtain to see a full house in attendance. He rubbed Lily's arm and said, "Sing, Little Bird, sing. I love you. You will be great." He took a deep breath, then walked to the center of the stage.

"Welcome, everyone. It is a great honor tonight to introduce my daughter, Lily Tucci. Tonight, she will perform Bach's 'Air on the G-String,' Chopin's 'Mysterious Forest,' with the finale of Debussy's 'Claire de Lune.' I give you Lily Tucci."

Lily walked onto the stage as everyone applauded. She calmed down when she heard the loud applause. It made her feel accepted. She stood by the piano and bowed, then sat on the bench seat. She took a deep breath, visualized the music in her head, and began to play. The music flowed through her body, down through her fingers, and onto the keys. Once finished, she stood and took a bow to the applauding audience. The second piece went just as well. Finally, "Claire de Lune" made Lily feel so tranquil and happy. She played it the best Lorenzo had ever heard, softly like a mother quietly singing a lullaby to her baby at bedtime. What made it so spectacular was that she ended gently; her music was a cloud slowly drifting away. The audience stood and wildly applauded. The boys whistled as they clapped. Women cried from the touching performance. Lily's Papa approached her and handed her a bouquet of red roses. She bowed once more with tears in her eyes.

Lorenzo led her off stage. "Do not cry, Little Bird. They loved you."

"I am overwhelmed by their response," she cried. "I am okay now." She wiped her tears away with her fingers.

"Let us go enjoy the party."

They met the family and staff at the party. The women's eyes were red from crying. Lily's playing had touched everyone. Everyone hugged and complimented her. The night was beyond her wildest dreams.

The party ended, and the little girls were exhausted. Lorenzo carried each to the bedroom and sat them down on the bed. "Now change and get a good night's sleep. I will see both of you in the morning." He kissed their foreheads then rubbed Lily's arm, "Sing, Little Bird, sing. I love you. You were fantastic. I am immensely proud of you. Goodnight."

"I love you, too, Papa."

The girls undressed but stayed in their underclothes, too tired to change. Tucked under the covers, they fell fast asleep.

Lorenzo quietly walked in and placed a vase with the roses on the coffee table. He admired the sweet, sleeping girls, then tiptoed from the room.

The family was sad to leave the next day. They'd had an enjoyable time. They loved the concert, activities, and food. After they left, Lily took a nap. She was still exhausted.

Lorenzo decided she needed to rest the next couple of months before starting a new program to practice. The three pieces he thought about were exceedingly difficult and would need more time. He chose Beethoven's "Moonlight Sonata," Bach's "Italian Concerto," and Liszt's "La Campanella." He thought the family needed to start taking vacations and have more fun time. He thought they would enjoy a trip down the Mississippi River on a paddle boat and maybe a trip to Canada to see Niagara Falls and Toronto. He thought Lily would love to go to Maine to catch lobsters and eat them and do whale watching. A trip to visit family for her birthday, with a Fourth of July celebration at Ida's, could be their final trip before her next concert in December 1893. Also, Sal needed time away from work. They needed time together.

Chapter 18

May 1892

Tallahassee, Florida

George found the perfect girl in an eighteen-year-old Sissy Tidewater after all those “other losers.” Brown hair, green eyes, five feet and four inches tall, shapely, and cute, the waitress at the local diner was not bright and exactly what he wanted. He enjoyed her fun personality. She even liked to party and drink. She cleaned his apartment, cooked, and made drinks for the guys when they came to play cards; and she did not mind him going to the pub with the guys for drinks every night. He would marry her once she bore him a son. No more fooling him. George was in his glory.

George sat at the table eating the delicious breakfast Sissy made before leaving for work. She was improving in her cooking. Thank goodness, thought George. He picked up the daily paper and was shocked. There on the front page was a photo of a new protégé, mother and father. No! It can't be! He exclaimed. That's my wife and the dump girl. They are making a fortune while I have been starving and trying to save up to get out of the hole.

He thought things through in his mind and decided to go to New York, follow them until they were alone then demand either money or they come home to make money for him. He read the article. So, they live in a plushy penthouse. This Lorenzo had millions of dollars.

Yes, he needed to stay in New York, follow them then when the chance comes to demand money. He finished his breakfast and put the dishes in the sink for Sissy to wash. He would go to the pub and plan. A couple of drinks would help him think.

The detective still followed George. A week later, George had found where Lorenzo Tucci lived. Everyone seemed to know him. Popular fellow. He found a cheap room to rent not too far away. He began to observe and follow their comings and goings for two weeks. No movement in the mornings except for a male or two. They seem to venture out in the afternoons to shop or visit an orphanage. They would lunch at an Italian restaurant that was too busy and large to get private with them. The Chinese restaurant was quaint and by the time they lunched the crowd had thinned out. The Chinese restaurant was it. The only problem now was the guy who drove them and acted like a bodyguard. He would wait for him to load the packages in the car to make his move.

George was enjoying following them, but he didn't realize someone was following him.

The detective reported back to Lorenzo two days after George settled in and was following the ladies. He was instructed to observe for now as talking to someone was not bad. He was only to intervene if threats, yelling, manhandling or a weapon was involved. He was to advise Ricardo so he would be of help if needed. If a problem arose, they were to restrain him and bring him directly to Lorenzo and Sal. After years of observing George, the detective deduced that action would be needed. He had to discuss this with Ricardo thoroughly.

A week later, Violet and Lily went to the millinery shop to buy threads, needles, ribbons, buttons, and fabrics. Ricardo started to carry out the packages as the ladies went to the Dragon Den to get a table for lunch. Mr. Cho Lin escorted them to a back corner table then brought them jasmine tea and would be back to take their order.

As they sipped their tea, a man quickly sat across from them. "Are you glad to see me?" He smirked.

"How did you find us?" inquired Violet.

"The front page of the daily newspaper. What a surprise! Now that your daughter is famous (he would never acknowledge her as his) and rich, I think I deserve some of it," George proclaimed.

No one could speak as the detective and Ricardo stood on each side of George. "You will come quietly with us or the police station." demanded the detective. "Ladies have lunch. Ricardo will be back shortly." Each man took an arm and escorted George out and brought him to Lorenzo and Sal to be dealt with.

Tears ran down Lily's face. Violet was in shock. "Is everything okay," asked Mr. Cho Lin.

"Yes. We will have our usual. Ricardo will be back shortly. Hold his order until he returns," replied Violet. He nodded and left.

Violet put her hand over Lily's, "It will be alright. Lorenzo and Sal will take care of everything. See, he even had a detective following George and we had Ricardo. He can't hurt us anymore."

Lily took out her handkerchief and wiped her tears but did not speak. All those bad thoughts about herself came flashing back. She held back her tears.

When Ricardo came back, Violet asked Mr. Cho Lin to box their lunch to go and explained that Lily didn't feel well. Once they arrived in the penthouse, Lily fled to her room. Violet would give her time to process today and tonight talk to her.

At the dinner table, Lily's body language told all. Lorenzo, Sal, and Violet's hearts broke. They knew she would need time and assurance. After grace, Lorenzo broke the silence, "George has been compensated and will not bother either of you again. I promise. I had a detective following him since you arrived, and he is still following George. He will not ever get close to either of you again. I said we would protect both of you and always will. " Lorenzo tried to reassure Lily. Lily nodded then pushed her food around her plate until everyone was done. No one ate much. She then fled to her room and cried into her pillow.

The door opened and Lorenzo walked in and sat next to her. As she sat up, Lorenzo cradled her in his arms. "Little bird, I am here to protect you, always. You are our treasure. You are worth more than all the money Sal and I have." He rubbed her back.

"I know Papa. I didn't expect to ever see him. It brought back all the hurt." She cried until she was drained and fell asleep. Lorenzo tucked her under the covers, kissed her forehead and said, "Sing, Little Bird, sing. I love you." He quietly left.

Lily had a weird feeling, so she woke up. There at her footboard was George. She was so scared she couldn't scream. He came around and dragged her out of bed. "You're going to work for me now." He pulled her out of bed then led her into the hallway. She knew if she screamed Lorenzo and Sal would save her. She had to be brave and strong. She took a deep breath and let out a blood curling scream as loud as she could. Out of their rooms, Lorenzo and Sal ran to her. Sal grabbed Lily and Lorenzo beat up George. Then Lorenzo and Violet joined them in a group hug.

"Lily. Are you okay? You were screaming in your sleep," her mother asked. Lily opened her eyes. It was all a dream. They saved her like yesterday. "I am sorry I woke you. It was just a bad dream but it ended well."

They noticed Lorenzo and Sal standing in the doorway. "We just wanted to make sure she was okay."

"Now, go back to sleep," Violet instructed and kissed Lily's forehead.

The next morning, Lily woke and realized that George couldn't hurt her anymore. She felt protected and loved. Lorenzo and Sal made sure of that. She dressed and went to have breakfast. Lorenzo, Sal, and Violet were eating breakfast. "Good morning, everyone. Sorry to disturb your sleep last night. Thank you all for your patience and understanding."

Lorenzo got up and went to hug her. "We love you, little bird. I think you need a couple of weeks off from so much excitement. Maybe Violet, she can help you at the orphanage. It might be good to get acquainted with other young ladies."

"That is a splendid idea. I need help anyways this afternoon. Several of the girls about your age want to make quilts for themselves. You can instruct them and get to know them. We will leave right after lunch. I am sure Sonata would love for you to play ball and teach her more commands this morning." said Violet.

Lily met the headmistress. She was delightful. Violet ushered Lily into a room with large windows that let in plenty of light for sewing. Sitting around a long, rectangular wooden table and chairs sat five young ladies of various ages. Violet introduced her to Tilda, Grace, Hannah, Betsy, and Molly. Violet placed the basket of supplies on the table by an empty seat for Lily. " I will let Lily instruct you how to sew these squares together to make larger squares then into your blanket. It will take a couple of months, but it will be worth it." She left the girls in Lily's capable hands.

The girls were quick learners. They got to know each other as they chatted about themselves. Two hours flew by. Violet came to collect Lily. The girls took turns hugging and thanking Lily for the lovely time. She made new friends. Violet promised the girls that Lily would return on Tuesday and Thursday afternoon until they finished their project.

On the way home, Lily asked if the girls could come for lunch sometime, and she could play the piano for them. Violet agreed that if Lily didn't have any more nightmares in three weeks, they would invite them to lunch. Lily agreed and felt more at peace with herself.

She had an occasional nightmare, but it ended with Sal and Lorenzo never letting her get past the hallway and always beating up on George. The last five days were nightmare free. After the two weeks, Lily was ready to practice. She missed playing but enjoyed her time off.

She was back to herself.

Chapter 19

Mid-July 1893

The Tucci family returned from Ida and Duncan's house. They had enjoyed being with family for a two-week vacation. Sonata was well behaved and had a fun time with King. Lily's sixteenth birthday was wonderful. The meal and the peach pie were excellent. She received perfume from Sal and Lorenzo, a basket of grooming products from Ida and Duncan, and a lovely piano-shaped music box that played "Swan Lake" from the Harris family. A Fourth of July picnic and fireworks made everyone excited and thankful to experience the holiday together.

The hot weather turned delightful and would be like that for the week. Violet and Lily decided to invite the girls from the orphanage for lunch in two days. Lorenzo hired two horse drawn carriages as transportation. Violet and Lily discussed with Mario what would be to their liking. They decided on lasagna, garlicky bread, and salad. His delicious and light lemon gelato with curled sugar cookie would be decadent. All was set.

They arrived at 12:30. They felt like Cinderella when entering the penthouse. Almost afraid to move and touch anything until Sonata ran to them bumping over a table with nick-nacks with a vase of flowers. Everyone laughed. The Marys proceeded to clean up the mess as Lily escorted them onto the terrace. They sat down and started to relax as they ate. Conversation covered Sonata, how Lily dealt with living in such a place and what she did. Once they were done eating, Lily brought them into the festivities room. She entertained them by playing the piano. They were so overwhelmed with her talent and applauded. She promised to get them tickets for her upcoming concert and to join the party after. They were excited and couldn't wait. They left and Lily felt very happy to have friends over.

August 1893

Their routine at home was back to normal. Before they sat down for lunch, Lorenzo came in with a young Englishman. "This is John Anderson. John, this is my sister Violet and my daughter Lily. You have met everyone else. Please have a seat and join us."

Lorenzo and John sat down. "John graduated from Harvard with a business and law degree and did his law internship at a prestigious law firm in New York City. Sal will instruct him in all aspects of his work until Christmas. After the New Year, I will instruct him in all of mine; he will need no more than three months. When I collaborate with John, I will practice with Lily for two hours three times a week. Then, it will be back to normal practice; I promise, Lily. We hope John will be able to take control if anything happens to one of us in the future. We plan later to hire two more people to help run the company." Lorenzo gave Lily his big, beautiful smile. She nodded back. She knew he would never forget her in his daily plans.

John sat across the table from Lily. He was awestruck by her beauty. He felt incredibly attracted to her. He should be careful, he knew; she was the boss's daughter.

Lily also felt something for John. Was it his English accent or his tall height or his sandy color hair or bright blue eyes or that muscular manly frame? Oh boy! She'd better take control of herself, or she would be in trouble. He worked for her papa, after all.

The looks Lily and John gave each other were observed by all. The next few months were going to be interesting.

"Sal, show John around and to his quarters. We all dine together in this dining room. Tonight, we will gather here at seven." Sal and John left.

"Lily, it is time for more practice. You have perfected "Moonlight Sonata," "Italian Concerto," and started "La Campanella." I think by Christmas all three pieces will be perfect. I will schedule December twenty-third for your second concert. Everyone will be here for Christmas. They will come in on the twenty-second, see the concert on the twenty-third, stay for Christmas Eve and Christmas Day, and leave after breakfast on the twenty-sixth."

"Violet, what are your plans?"

"I am meeting with the committee to help the orphanage I started last year. We will get a list of needs and wants from the headmistress and go from there. There are needs all year round. We have thirty members already!"

"Sounds like everyone is busy."

October 1893

Before Lily would get too busy, she wanted to take the girls to lunch at the Dragon Den then back to the penthouse to play cards. They loved the decorations and food. They loved playing cards and laughed a lot. It was a nice break before she worked hard.

December 1893

Everyone came to New York City on December twenty-second. Lorenzo introduced their new member, John, to everyone as they arrived. All were glad Sal and Lorenzo were getting help. This would allow more time for themselves and for family. John was great with the boys, which impressed the women. Lorenzo took everyone to the Dragon Den for dinner. He reserved the whole restaurant for his large party. Mr. Cho Lin asked what soup each one preferred, then the rest of the meal was family style. He served egg rolls with duck sauce, fried wontons, fried rice, six different traditional dishes, and two spicy dishes. After their meal, the table was cleared to make room for hot Jasmine tea and Mr. Cho Lin's famous almond cookies.

The next day, the concert was beyond Lorenzo's dreams. The headmistress and girls attended the concert and were awed. The after-party was the best ever. They felt honored to have Lily as a friend and to be included. Lily felt everything was surreal. She was happy the girls enjoyed everything and shared her moment.

The party was wonderful. This time, she was able to relax and enjoy the event. She had an odd feeling that John was watching her. His attention gave her a tingly feel. John could not take his eyes off Lily. She was like a siren calling to him. He needed to find out if she felt something for him before he would pursue her.

Christmas was full of gifts, food, games, rides, snow activities, and skating. Family gatherings were not only fun but also exhausting. Everyone needed a couple of days after to recoup.

Chapter 20

January 1894

After New Year's Eve, Lorenzo let Lily rest a couple of weeks before he gave her the three new pieces to practice. He selected Antonin Dvorak's- "Slavonic Dance," Johann Strauss's "Tales from the Vienna Woods," then a duet of Lily and Lorenzo playing Tchaikovsky's "Swan Lake." These three pieces would create a lovely evening of waltzes. He would touch base for two hours three times a week. Their tutoring time would be back to normal by the end of March. Violet would attend Lily's practices and advise as needed.

Lily's mind was composing music describing her life. Lily had a great idea and discussed it with Violet. She planned to create her own composition and dedicate it in honor of her Papa. Violet was excited to help. Lily would practice her concert in the morning and compose with Violet's piano secretly in the afternoons. Lily envisioned a storm building in the lower keys with a sporadic flicking of the upper keys like a chirping sound. Once the storm hit its' peak, she transitioned into a frolicking melody in the lower keys with the same chirping sound in the upper keys. She transitioned again into a tranquil melody in the lower keys accompanied by a twittering melody in the upper keys as though a bird were singing. For the finale, with her right fingers, she quickly ran across the upper keys as if the bird were taking flight. Simple but expressive. This was her life in a melody. She wanted Lorenzo to know she could now sing and fly away. Violet and Lily were ecstatic about her composition.

April fast approached. Lorenzo and Lily were back together full time in the practice room. He announced the third concert would be on Valentine's Day. He decided that having it during Christmas was additional work and stress. They would have more time to enjoy family visits and let Lily progress at a more comfortable pace with a February date.

Lorenzo worked with Lily in fine tuning "Slavonic Dance." By June, she dove into playing "Tales from the Vienna Woods."

The family took a break and vacationed the last week of June and the first week of July to see Ida and Duncan. The family get-togethers were needed and celebrations made them memorable.

Sonata was happy to be included on their trip. She was great at traveling and did not mind where they stayed. Lorenzo and Sal left John in charge in

New York. They found upon their return that John did an excellent job and managed several new situations well. They were now inquiring to hire two more men into their company.

Lily needed a break and decided to invite the girls for lunch and a game of crochet on the terrace. They had a great time and caught up with all the news. Crochet was a hit. Lily would tell Lorenzo to buy a set for them for Christmas from her. They certainly noticed the gorgeous young man watching them from the terrace doorway for a few minutes. They wanted the low-down on him. Lily gave a condensed response. They all guessed Lily had eyes for him, herself.

September arrived. Lily and Lorenzo started practicing their duet. Lorenzo had taken everyone last year to see the ballet version of *Swan Lake*. The women cried. Even Lorenzo's eyes had moistened. Knowing the music, Lily became excited and nervous. She loved her Papa, but he was such a perfectionist. Could she play up to his standards? She hoped she could. Lily enjoyed the waltzes. They were lively and carefree. They made one happy. The song "Swan Lake" was an exception—not carefree but dramatic. They sat side by side on the piano bench. Lorenzo played while Lily's left hand crossed under Lorenzo's right hand and her right hand to the right of Lorenzo's. Then, Lorenzo played the lower keys as Lily played the upper keys. Lily had the main melody. Sometimes, their pinkies barely touched. It took five days of diligent practice before they were coordinated.

"I love this piece. It has become my favorite," exclaimed Lily.

"It is mine as well. The song is emotional. We did great. Finding how to place your hands is the tricky part. If you played the piece yourself, it would be a lot easier," explained Lorenzo.

"I am exhausted and need a snack. I will take Sonata to the terrace and play ball with her. She and I need the exercise and fresh air."

They went up the elevator. As they exited the elevator, the detective and Sal greeted them. The man nodded to them, entered the elevator, and was gone. Sonata ran to Lily then sat, with a ball in her mouth. Lily patted Sonata's head. "I know you want to play."

"I hope practice went well," asked Sal.

"It was challenging but fun," replied Lily. "I will be off to the kitchen then to the terrace. See you at dinner." Lily patted Sonata's head then led Sonata towards the kitchen, "Let me get a snack first."

Sal and Lorenzo turned and walked to their offices to continue working.

Lily poured a glass of lemonade, placed a couple of cookies on a dish, then placed the glass and dish on a small tray Mario handed her. She went to set the tray on one of the terrace tables. Sonata, knowing the routine, followed Lily with a ball secured in his mouth. John sat reading a book with a glass of lemonade at one of the tables near him. He heard someone coming, then looked up.

"I hope we will not disturb you. Sonata barks a lot when playing ball," asked Lily.

John stood up, "Not at all." He rubbed Sonata's neck. "Please join me." He took her tray and placed it on the table opposite his seat.

"Just until I finish my snack. Sonata wants to play ball. We have a routine. She lets me snack while she sniffs out anything new. Then we play."

John helped with her chair then sat across from her. James arrived and said, "I thought you would care for more lemonade and cookies." He placed a pitcher of lemonade and a plate of cookies in the center of the table.

"Thank you, James. You are always so thoughtful," said John.

"It is my job sir. Do you require anything else?" asked James.

"No. We are all set," said Lily.

James left them alone. As he entered the dining room, he saw Violet seated at the table, facing the terrace, and watching the young couple as a chaperone. "Would you care for some tea and cookies, madam?" asked James.

"That would be lovely, James. Could I please have my tea with lemon?" asked Violet.

"Right away, madam," he turned to watch the two play catch with Sonata. He turned and went to get Violet her snack. She was still playing chaperone when he placed her tea and cookies on the table. "They make a lovely couple, if I may say so."

"Yes, they do," replied Violet dreamily. Then, James disappeared.

Violet was watching the couple when Sal and Lorenzo sat beside her. "What is so interesting?" asked Lorenzo.

"Young love, I believe," replied Violet. "I now see what you saw in him. I am beginning to like him."

James brought in coffee for the men and cookies. “Madam, would you care for more hot tea?”

“Yes, thank you.” James was quick and brought her tea with lemon then left the chaperones to do their duties.

“Lily is seventeen years old and at marriage age. John is seven years older, has established himself, and has a lot of money. His family owns a castle in England, but he acts kind and down to earth, like you and I do. When I interviewed him, I liked him right away. By my standards, he was professionally qualified for his position and actually fit my list of men I might want Lily to marry. Those were the primary reasons I hired him. I had hoped this might happen.”

“Oh, Lorenzo! How could you!” she laughingly slapped him on the shoulder. “But I am glad you did. I hope you are right. I was dreading the thought of escorting her to those awful coming out balls. It is like a meat market, and you still do not know who you are getting.”

Sal cleared his throat then spoke, “Violet, I just had a visit from the detective following George.” He paused. “I am afraid George has died. I did not want to discuss this in front of Lily. I do not think she needs to know.”

"Oh my! I agree with you. He is dead to her anyway. What happened?" inquired Violet.

"There was a pub fight. He was punched, fell back, hit his head on the counter, then fell to the floor. No one noticed him until the police arrived and found him dead on the floor."

"I am sorry for what happened to him. But at the same time, I am relieved. I can close that chapter in my life," Violet said sadly.

They continued to watch in silence until half an hour later. Lily was gathering up their trays and handed them to John to carry to the kitchen. Sonata had the ball in her mouth. Lily was placing the chairs back. The three elders had disappeared before Lily and John walked inside. They entered the penthouse not knowing they were ever watched.

That night, James served lasagna, a tossed salad, and garlic bread. Dessert was cannoli and peach pie. Lily looked at Lorenzo while eating her peach pie. When did he start getting white hair? Laugh lines? Wrinkles in his hands? She looked at Sal. When did dust cover his hair? Laugh lines? Wrinkles? She looked at her mother. She looked more mature but not old. There were no signs of white, but she saw a few laugh lines and wrinkles. She thought, *They are getting older and so am I. How does time pass by so quickly?*

Lorenzo got up and stated he was going to bed early due to a terribly busy work schedule tomorrow, so there would not be any practice. It was the first time he had ever shown he was tired. He kissed the ladies goodnight, said he loved them, and left.

"Do you think he is okay?" asked Lily.

"I do not know," answered Violet. "What do you think Sal?"

"He has a lot on his plate this week and some bad situations that need to be resolved. I would not put too much into it right now. We will see how he is in a week," guessed Sal. Sal left quickly after Lorenzo.

John came up to Violet. "Violet, as Sal and Lorenzo will be busy all day tomorrow, may I take you ladies out to lunch at your favorite restaurant?"

"That would be lovely. What do you say, Lily?" asked Violet with a sly smile.

Lily blushed. She knew her mothers' thoughts, "I would love to go."

"We can meet in the foyer at noon," instructed John. John left with a little skip to his steps.

“So, Lily, what do you think of John?” inquired Violet.

“I have grown to have feelings for him,” answered Lily.

Violet hugged her. Her daughter had grown up right in front of her eyes and she had not noticed until today. “He is considered a great catch, just as you are. Take this slowly, and do not let this relationship interfere with your work.”

“I will not. I love my work too much.”

Violet hugged her daughter, “I love you.”

“I love you, too.”

Chapter 21

A week later, John asked the ladies to take a carriage ride, and Lorenzo joined them. John got the message. Two weeks later, John asked the whole family to attend the opera. Lily and John sat between Lorenzo and Violet. All was proper. The outings were weekly. The interactions on the terrace happened three times a week, each time with a chaperone attending at the dining room table then quickly disappearing.

The family was invited to an annual ball on New Year's Eve. This was the first time anyone had accepted an invitation other than a select few fundraisers. Violet informed Sal and Lorenzo that she and Lily did not know how to dance. The men started to teach Lily and Violet steps to several dances each night. Four days later, Lorenzo bought a phonograph, which was delightful to hear and helped with getting the rhythm to their steps. They decided to add dancing to their Christmas fun and teach the steps to those who did not know how to dance. John would watch them from a darkened doorway. He saw how quickly Lily progressed and how the music flowed through her soul. Like playing the piano, she obviously loved dancing. He watched how Lorenzo gave up his role of dance partner to Lily after a couple of days. Sal was now her partner, and Lorenzo danced with Violet. John could not wait to dance with Lily at Christmas and hold her in his arms.

Before everyone arrived at Christmas, John gave Lily a lovely heart-shaped locket with his painted picture inside. As they sat on the terrace together, she could only express that she loved the gift. Lily had John clasp it around her neck. Working the clasp, John's fingertips lightly grazed Lily's neck. Their touch sent a tingly sensation to her neck and to his fingertips. That was the first time they had had any type of physical contact.

Christmas was filled with activities and food. The gifts were special and thoughtful. The boys loved their time with Uncle Sal. The girls had a great time with Lorenzo. Savanah noticed John staying near Lily and the looks John and Lily gave each other. "So, what is the story with John?" asked Savanah one night during a late bedroom talk.

"I am falling in love with John. He is courting me as much as Sal and Lorenzo will let him. He gave me this lovely locket with his picture inside," replied Lily as she opened the locket to show Savanah.

"Does he have a brother I may have?" she laughed.

"Sorry, no. I know you will find the right person soon because you are terrific," assured Lily.

"I have found someone, but he does not know it. I have had my eye on Tom's best friend, Jeffrey. He is so dreamy. I am slowly talking and flirting with him. I even went out caroling with someone from my class to make him jealous. I have watched the girls work on my brothers, so I know a few tricks. I will write and let you know how things are progressing," stated Savanah.

Dancing was added every night to the Christmas activities. Surprisingly, the boys were interested and did well. Girls were on the boys' minds and holding one in their arms sounded great. Everyone switched partners, and John finally was able to hold Lily. Heat radiated from John and made Lily feel a need to get closer to him. This was not permitted. After the dance, John excused himself and went outside. He had to cool his reaction to Lily.

Christmas went quickly. Everyone had another wonderful time. Everyone also wondered what new activity Sal and Lorenzo would devise for next year.

New Year's Eve
1895

The ball was like a fairy tale to Lily. The ballgowns were beautiful. The ballroom of their host and hostess was decorated in gold and silver with black accents. The orchestra sounded like a dream. Lily saw visions in her mind with each piece played, which caused her to miss her footing occasionally. Several young men asked for a dance, which she was obligated to accept whether she wanted to or not, unless it was the second time. The rule was never to accept a second dance unless engaged or married to the man. Lily was the most popular single lady that evening. She was stunning in her royal blue gown, and it did not hurt that she was now rich. John would marry her even if she wore rags and was dirt poor. He loved her that much. Tomorrow, these wolves would be calling on her and sending her gifts endeavoring to court her. He could not wait any longer.

Lily watched all the young ladies fawn over John. Their behavior made her jealous. What was wrong with her? The young men were nice to her and she found a couple of them attractive, but they were not John. On the ride home, Lorenzo asked

Lily if she was interested in any of the young gentlemen she met, as they would be calling upon her tomorrow. She replied that she was not. Violet, Sal, and Lorenzo gave an all-knowing smile. John just grunted.

The very next morning after breakfast, Lily took Sonata to play ball on the terrace. John asked Sal, Lorenzo, and Violet if he could privately speak to them. He wanted to do this before those peacocks came calling. The three knew what this was about and escorted him to Lorenzo's office for their talk.

All sat but John. He nervously paced, then finally faced them. "I have grown to love Lily with all my heart. I want to protect her, nurture her, be her partner in all things, and love her for the rest of our lives. I would like your permission to have the honor of marrying Lily," John held his breath for their reply.

They all jumped up and hugged him and in unison said" Yes!"

"Welcome to the family!" said Violet.

"About time," replied Sal.

"When would you like to get married?" asked Lorenzo.

"Two months after her concert, in May," responded John gleefully.

"The Saturday after Mother's Day would be perfect," added Violet.

Lorenzo put on a concerned face and asked, "Would you have Lily stop doing her concerts?"

"I would not want her to stop. She might stop when we have a baby. I am sure she would start sometime after," assured John.

All smiled for that was what they needed to know.

"I had better get back to Lily. I will tell her you have a meeting and will collaborate with her after lunch. I am sure you men have a lot to talk about," Violet hugged John then left.

"Violet, tell James we will not be receiving any visitors today," winked Sal.

"Oh, I forgot about them. I better do that quickly," laughed Violet.

"I was not looking forward to this morning with visitor after visitor. Please sit, John, and let us discuss a few things before we need to get back to work," said Lorenzo.

"When do you plan on proposing?" asked Sal.

"At the party after her concert."

"Do you have a ring?" asked Lorenzo.

"I have not picked one out yet."

"Perfect," said Lorenzo. "Tomorrow, we will go to my jeweler. You may pick out whatever you want. You need to pick out wedding bands, too. After, we will go to my favorite restaurant to celebrate."

"The Dragon Den?" asked John.

"Oh no! That is the lady's favorite. Mine is Antonio's Italian restaurant. Do not tell Mario, but Antonio cooks a couple of my favorite dishes that Mario cannot make."

"I will tell Lily we cannot practice tomorrow due to an out of the office meeting for us all. Everyone understand the plan?"

They nodded yes.

"After you are engaged, call me Papa," requested Lorenzo.

"Call me Uncle Sal," requested Sal. "And welcome to the family."

The next day, John, Sal, and Lorenzo were driven by Ricardo to Mr. Goldmann's jewelry shop. John explained the design he wanted for the engagement ring and gave him one of Lily's gloves

Violet had given him in order to get the ring size right.

"I can make that for you by the end of the week. One carat oval with heart shape rubies on each side. A gold setting in a filagree pattern that will butt up to the gold wedding bands."

"Yes, perfect."

"Can you design a necklace to match, but not too big?" asked Lorenzo. "I want it as a wedding gift for my daughter."

"No problem. I will have everything ready by the end of the week," answered Mr. Goldmann.

The men went to the restaurant and were greeted and ushered by Antonio to a table in a back corner. The restaurant's décor was upscale. "Antonio, this my future son-in-law, John."

"Nice to meet you. What would everyone like to drink?" asked Antonio as he passed out the menus.

"Bring us your special chianti. The bill is all on me," said Lorenzo.

"I will be right back."

"John let me order for you. If you do not like what I choose, you can choose something else," said Lorenzo.

"Yes, please. There is so much on the menu, I cannot decide," said John.

Antonio came back and poured the glasses of wine then spoke in Italian to ask for their order. He gathered the menus then left. Lorenzo toasted to the happiness to Lily and John. Italian wedding soup was served to Ricardo and Sal. John and Lorenzo had a delicious mushroom soup. Next, everyone had an Italian salad. Ricardo and Sal were served Braciole (stuffed meat rolls) with pasta and eggplant parmesan. A breadbasket full of warm garlic bread was placed in the center of the table. John and Lorenzo's dishes had steamed clams, mussels, shrimp, and scallops tossed with a lemon garlic pesto sauce topped with finely chopped tomatoes over linguini then sprinkled with Romano cheese and crushed red hot peppers.

John tasted his meal then moaned, "Have I died and gone to heaven? This is delicious."

"Thank you," Antonio beamed.

"Why do the ladies not prefer Antonio's?" asked John.

"They prefer Mario's cooking, or they do not want to hurt his feelings. It is anyone's guess," answered Sal.

The table was cleared. Then Antonio placed before each man a plate with a slice of Italian cheesecake topped with chocolate sauce. “This is on the house to celebrate your new son-in-law.”

“Thank you, Antonio. Everything is delicious. No wonder your restaurant is Lorenzo’s favorite. It has now become mine as well,” complimented John.

Chapter 22

February 1894

People would be arriving any minute. Time was going fast, but not for John. Lily had not seen or talked with John much since the ball. After the concert, she needed answers to find out if something was wrong. She heard Sonata barking and realized the guests had arrived. Lorenzo announced dinner would be at Antonio's and the Dragon Den tomorrow, so Mario had time to prepare the food for after the concert. Sal and Lorenzo excused themselves to finish business before they went out to dinner.

The adults went into the parlor for finger sandwiches and tea while the children went into the festivities room to play with Sonata, play games, and snack.

Several cars ferried the group to Antonio's. Lorenzo reserved a private room. Everyone loved the food, but the women confessed to loving Mario's better. Mario thought the food was just as good and loved their compliments.

That night, Lorenzo came to say goodnight. He kissed the girls' foreheads, rubbed Lily's arm, then said, "Sing, Little Bird, sing. I love you."

“I love you, too, Papa.” Lily felt better. Lorenzo was back to his old self. She could sleep now.

The next morning after breakfast, Lorenzo and Lily went to practice on stage. All except Lorenzo and Sal went to the Dragon’s Den. They needed to finish business for the day. No one thought it was strange, as more time was taken away from their business due to Lorenzo performing with Lily. As usual, everyone knew the routine except this time John was included. Everyone was excited for the duet. They were in for a big surprise!

Lorenzo introduced Lily then announced the program with the finale as a duet with Lily and himself. Everyone became silent in anticipation of the concert. The first two pieces received standing ovations. Now came the icing on the cake. Everyone held their breath until the music began. The two started to play; fingers and hands flew. The music was so moving that there was not a dry eye in the building. “Encore!” was yelled many times to no avail. Lily and Lorenzo hugged each other once off stage.

“That was amazing, Papa!” cried Lily. "Sorry the girls got colds and missed out."

“Yes, it was. Let us go celebrate with everyone.”

They took the elevator upstairs. Flowers, food, and beverages were everywhere. John watched from afar as the family embraced Lily's success. Lorenzo gave a touching toast to having a fantastic concert.

John became nervous. This was his moment. Would she say yes or no? He started to walk towards her. Violet took the glass from Lily's hand, "Let me freshen this for you."

Lily turned from her mother and saw John walking straight for her. Suddenly, she felt nervous. What was he doing?

John walked up to Lily like a man with a mission. He got down on one knee, equipped with the ring in his right hand.

He wanted everyone to hear him, so he spoke loudly, "I love you with all my heart. I cannot live another day without you by my side. Lily Mae Tucci, will you do me the honor of becoming my wife?" He did it without faltering and awaited her response.

Lily felt she was in a fairy tale with a young prince before her. Nervous and excited, she listened to him speak. His voice sent chills down her spine. This was why he had avoided her. He was proposing to her in front of everyone! "It would be my honor to accept your proposal. I love you, too," replied Lily with a big grin.

John placed the ring on her finger. It fit perfectly. He appreciated Violet's suggestion to use Lily's glove to get the ring sized. "It is beautiful, John. I love my ring," exclaimed Lily.

"I designed it myself. I had hoped you would like the heart-shaped rubies," proclaimed John. He was now allowed to kiss her. He slowly leaned toward her lips. Lily could not believe they were finally going to kiss. Their lips softly met. It was electrifying! They felt they were on fire. The kiss told them it was right. Everyone came to congratulate them, which quickly ended the kiss. Ida and Carolyn were mad at Violet for not telling them when they arrived but soon forgave her. Wedding plans would take place after everyone left.

Chapter 23

The next day, everyone left happy and exhausted. During lunch, the family and John discussed the wedding plans. It was decided the Saturday after Mother's Day would be the day for the wedding. This gave John's family time to get ready to travel across the Atlantic to attend. A minister and friend of Lorenzo's would perform the ceremony at 10:00 AM in their ballroom. A reception line would be set up in the everyday dining room followed by a brunch in the formal dining room (the table seated fifty people, so there was plenty of room). John's family would have the suites on John's floor. They would eat with the family except on the morning before the wedding. James would bring to their suite's coffee, tea, and biscuits to tide them over them until brunch.

Next week, Violet, Sal, Lily, Lorenzo, and John would visit the florist, stationery shop, Rosa's Bakery and Café to order the cake and pastries and wedding favors, city hall for the license, and the minister's office to go over the ceremony. The second day, Violet and Lily would go to the dressmaker for a fitting. Besides a wedding dress, Lily needed a trousseau for her honeymoon. Violet needed something special to wear to her daughter's wedding. The third day, Sal, Lorenzo, John, Ricardo, James, and Mario would go to the tailor to be fitted for their morning clothes.

The happy couple decided they would travel back to England with his family and honeymoon there. They could take day trips, do activities on the grounds, and stay with his Aunt Tess, Uncle Albert, and Bert in London for a few days to sightsee, shop, and take in a play or concert or musical. Lily could do some practicing at his parent's castle and on the ship. They wanted to live with everyone in the penthouse when they returned. The idea was overwhelmingly accepted. Lorenzo and Sal would redecorate Violet's room for the happy couple and turn Lily's room into Violet's room. Both rooms would be done by the time they came back in September.

Lorenzo asked Lily if she would like to plan the next concert. She was thrilled to accept his offer. This is when she could play her composition for him. It was decided the concert would be held on Valentine's Day, the best date for all. He asked if she planned to continue giving concerts. She would continue but would take a break whenever she became pregnant. All was good.

The next day, Sal introduced two new employees. “Colin Frazer, Scotsman, and a graduate from Harvard in business and law. His family in Scotland owns a whisky and mead distillery. Next, Jovani Gambini is the grandson of the Gambini family. We stayed with the Gambini’s when we came to America. He is also a graduate of Harvard in accounting and law.”

Sal introduced everyone around the table. Sal would train them, then Lorenzo would take over after the wedding until just before the couple came back.

Sal and Lorenzo were getting older. Lily worried their work was becoming too much to manage. Lily was relieved when they hired more help. Now, she could enjoy her honeymoon without worries.

Chapter 24

John's parents, Diana, and John, Sr., with his grandmother Lacy, his Aunt Tess, his Uncle Albert, and their son Bert, would arrive two days before the wedding. Lily's family would be coming three days before to deter chaos.

Lily's family arrived all excited. Lily took Savanah to the dressmaker to be fitted for a maid of honor dress. It was Lily's treat. Aunt Ida, Aunt Carolyn, and Violet came along. The dressmaker found a beautiful pink fabric with white lily of the valley blooms scattered across the hem. She advised adding a white sash at the waist to liven the look. Violet had picked a red dress with white lace trim. The dresses would be delivered early the morning of the wedding to prevent wrinkling, and she would make sure nothing needed her attention and was perfect. Afterwards, the ladies enjoyed lunch at the Dragon's Den, did some shopping, and finished at Rosa's Bakery and Café for high tea.

The next day, John's family arrived. They loved Lily right away and made Lily feel like a family member. John asked his father to be best man. All the men went to get John, Sr., fitted for his morning attire. After, the men lunched at Antonio's.

Everyone got along like they knew each other and were family.

Sonata was enjoying all the attention, especially from the boys. Jasper had trained her well. He would oversee her during this week and the couple of months while the couple was on their honeymoon. The next few weeks would be chaotic and could cause Sonata to be upset. He was to keep her calm and happy.

Mario outdid himself with the rehearsal dinner. He served roasted leg of lamb with mint jelly and roasted potatoes, prime rib with Yorkshire pudding, lasagna with Mario's special spread on Italian bread slices, brussels sprouts with water chestnuts, orange glazed carrots, buttered green beans, tossed salad with a berry vinaigrette dressing, and rolls. For dessert, he made strawberry shortcake, peach pie, Tiramisu, and an English chocolate date torte. Even the boys were stuffed. After their delicious meal, Aunt Ida played a few songs for a sing-along. Then, all retired for a good night's sleep so they would be ready by 9:30 AM for the big day.

Besides family, there would be friends of Sal and Lorenzo, a few ladies from Violet's charity work, their staff, Rosa, Antonio, Mr. Cho Lin, Mr.

Goldmann, the florist, the tailor, the seamstress, as well as the headmistress and the girls.

The wedding day was here. Everyone was busy getting ready. The men chose well. Black, full-length morning coats, white shirts with black studs and buttons, red and white striped ties, red brocade vests, and black and white, thin-striped trousers made them look dapper. Uncle Albert and Bert were smartly dressed in their formal morning attire as well. No hats or gloves were required for the indoor ceremony. James brought in the red rose boutonnieres for all the men to complete their look. James brought Tom and Duncan each a boutonniere. The men were taken care of, so next were the ladies flowers.

James knocked on the door then entered once invited. He carried a large box and set it on the chaise lounge chair, then quickly left. Violet's red dress, Diana's green dress, Aunt Tess's rose dress, and Lacy's floral dress went perfectly with the corsage of lilies of the valley surrounding a red rose. Savanah picked up a bouquet of lilies of the valley embraced by a white doily with long white streaming ribbons. Lily's bouquet consisted of four red roses (representing Violet, Sal, Lorenzo, and Lily) in the center, surrounded by lily of the valley blossoms. Embracing the flowers were green ferns then a white doily, giving the bouquet a delicate look. The flowers were perfect.

Violet and Savanah helped Lily into her Italian lace dress that was adorned with pearls and crystals. Matching headband of pearls and crystals held her Italian lace veil in place. She wore the necklace Sal and Lorenzo gave her this morning as a wedding gift. She looked breathtaking.

Rosa came at 7:00 AM to set up the cake on a round table in the corner of the dining room. She placed cookies, pastries, and white candied almonds wrapped in netting (wedding favors) around the cake. Once finished, she helped Mario. The florist arrived about the same time. After giving James instructions on the boxes of flowers to hand out, she proceeded to decorate the rooms with flowers and bows. At 9:20 AM, the minister arrived and helped James greet and direct the guests. The Andersons arrived at 9:25 AM and were directed to where they should go. Ida started to play tranquil music at 9:25 AM until it was time for the event to begin.

At 9:55 AM, Lorenzo entered Lily's bedroom. "Little Bird, you look stunning. Let us make this happen, unless you have second thoughts," asked Lorenzo.

"Oh, Papa! I am ready!" replied Lily.

When Ida saw Violet and Sal at the doorway, she stopped playing the current song and started playing Pachelbel's "Canon in D." Violet and Sal walked down the aisle then took their seats. Next, John, Sr., and Savanah walked down the aisle and stood by the minister. Then all rose as Lorenzo escorted Lily down the aisle to John.

The music stopped once all were in place. The minister asked, "Who gives this woman to this man?"

Lorenzo replied, "Her mother and I." Violet was touched that Lorenzo included her in his response. He lifted Lily's veil and kissed her forehead.

Ida started to play "Ave Maria" by Schubert, and Lorenzo, with his tenor voice, sweetly sang. This was a surprise gift. When finished singing, Lorenzo sat beside Violet. Vows were exchanged.

Violet rose to read scripture then sat down. Rings were exchanged. Lorenzo stood up and sang as Ida started to play "O Promise Me" by Reginald De Koven and Clement Scott. Many became teary eyed.

The minister pronounced them man and wife. Finally, they were able to kiss. What a kiss! Ida played Mendelssohn's "Wedding March" as the couple started down the aisle. They were followed by family and guests.

The reception line went slowly but did not take too long. The brunch was unbelievable. Mr. Cho Lin brought his eggrolls with duck sauce, and Antonio brought antipasto platters. The three-tiered wedding cake was the center of everyone's attention. The bottom consisted of three layers of Italian lemon sponge cake with cannoli filling. The second tier consisted of three layers of chocolate cake filled with chocolate mouse and maraschino cherries. The top tier consisted of three layers of yellow amaretto cake filled with pastry cream and berries. The outside was coated with white buttercream frosting and decorated with marzipan red roses, lilies of the valley, and green ferns. At the top center rested a bouquet of the same flowers surrounded by ferns. Shell edging was piped at the bottom and top edges. The cake was a work of art but unbelievably delicious. Everyone had to have a slice of each layer.

Guests left by 2:15 PM. Everyone changed clothes then finished packing. By 4:00 PM, Ricardo and other drivers had loaded the luggage. Everyone said their goodbyes and wished the lovely couple a safe trip. Sal hugged John. While Lorenzo hugged

John, he whispered in his ear, "You had better love and take good care of Lily or there will be consequences." At first, John was taken back, but he thought if he had a daughter, he would do the same and took no offense.

Lorenzo hugged Lily and whispered in her ear, "I love you, Little Bird. Be happy. We will miss you until you return home."

"I love you, too, Papa," Lily replied and kissed his cheek. Lily was sad to leave her family but was excited to start another journey with John. They left at 4:15 PM.

The adults were exhausted and retired to their bedrooms for naps. Savanah and Sonata lay on Lily's bed while recalling the day as Savanah slowly fell asleep. The boys played on the terrace. They had plates of cookies and pastries with milk to keep them busy. Mario felt mitigated in hiring a staff to help with preparations, clear, and to clean everything and rooms up. Once all was done to his satisfaction, he, too, was exhausted and took a nap. For once, leftovers were dinner.

Chapter 25

Lily and John had the best suite on the ship in first class thanks to his aunt and uncle—their wedding gift. Chilled champagne and chocolates were on the coffee table and arrived every night. John's family left the couple alone during the day. They would meet his family for dinner and dancing at night except the first and last three nights. During the day, Lily practiced in the grand ballroom while John read books from the ship's library. John had arranged lunch to be delivered to the ballroom so Lily could take a break at any time.

Their first intimate time together, Lily experienced, as expected, some blood loss but little pain. This was due to John's patience and techniques. Their lovemaking was beyond their expectations. They could not get enough of each other. After dancing and until after breakfast in bed, they were sequestered in their cabin. They enjoyed a great start to their honeymoon.

Lily soon caught her first glimpse of Dover, England. The tall white cliffs were impressive, with birds flying everywhere. Several drivers waited for them on the dock and would take them and their luggage to the train station. The Andersons arranged a train ride with lunch on board to Tunbridge Wells station. The train ride was delightful. The scenery was breathtaking. The food was delectable. Drivers greeted them at their stop, loaded their luggage, and then drove them directly to the castle. The Andersons' estate included 278 acres surrounding Scotney Castle. As a fully working estate, it contained a large staff and many small cottages and rooms in the castle to house them. As they approached the estate, sheep were seen grazing in beautiful fields with various floral patches here and there. The castle had a small moat with swans and lily pads that flowed around two thirds of the castle. Once Lily saw the castle as more of a country manor than a frightening huge castle, she was relieved. A variety of flowers and greenery created a soft kaleidoscope of colors everywhere. A stone bridge featured the moat to the right, and on the left sat a pond. The land sprawled and rolled outward in green. They drove across the bridge and arrived at a circular driveway with a large fountain in the center. Staff awaited their arrival. Lily could see herself retired and old living here. The grounds were a tranquil and fairy-like setting.

John's mother Diana had redecorated John's bedroom in yellows, whites, and greens to make it cheery. Fresh assorted flowers were placed to add a welcome and homey feeling. The Andersons let the maid and groomsman unpack for the couple. Diana wanted Lily to tour the house and surrounding grounds. Everyone except Lacy used the tour to stretch their legs, enjoy breaths of fresh air, and relax before dressing for dinner. Lacy needed a good hot cup of tea and a nap in her own bed.

The next day after breakfast, Lily felt right at home when she entered a parlor housing a grand piano! There was a blazing fire in the fireplace to make the room cozy. Lily found Lacy engulfed in a large leather wing chair by the fireplace with a lap blanket. “I hope I am not bothering your practice being here?” inquired Lacy in a soft voice.

“Not at all. I hope I am not bothering your quiet time?”

“Dear child, music fills my soul. It never did anything for either of my children. They accomplished social etiquette but never the proper social skills of music. I was very accomplished. If I were young, I could be professional like you in piano and voice. I may be old now, but I can quickly maneuver these bony fingers like lightening.”

They both laughed.

“What are you playing?”

"Pachelbel's 'Canon in D,' a new American composition called 'Amazing Grace,' and my composition for my Papa called 'Sing, Little Bird, Sing.'"

"I cannot wait for you to play! Please give this old lady something wonderful to finally listen to!"

"Yes. I hope you will approve of my playing," Lily responded. She took the bench and played "Canon in D."

"You are incredibly talented, Lily. Not everyone can express emotion in their craft," said Lacy.

"The next piece, 'Amazing Grace,' will be sung by a soulful opera type singer. Unfortunately, she is black and is not accepted in the professional circuit. I am taking a chance having people to hear her at our venue. I am afraid some will leave," sadly said Lily.

"Good for you Lily. If someone leaves, it will be his loss."

"I like to sing the words as I play because they are very powerful," added Lily. "I would love your critique after I finish."

Lily began. Her voice was lovely but not professional. She finished and looked up to see Lacy's face. Tears were running down the elderly woman's cheeks. She held a handkerchief in hand and tried to wipe them away.

"That was the most beautiful piece I have ever heard. Please play that at my funeral."

"My Uncle Duncan plays the bagpipes, and the song sounds even better with them. I will remember your request."

"I can hear it already. Eerie and peaceful at once."

"Now, for my composition. I hope you like it as well."

When Lily finished, Lacy was right beside her. She hugged Lily and kissed the top of her head. "We are two adults with one soul. Thank you for coming into our lives. Johnny is blessed. Excuse me, but I must rest before dinner." She left Lily feeling blessed as well.

Lily spent several hours practicing, always with Lacy in attendance. She left a day here and there or several afternoon hours to fish, sightsee, go horseback riding, attend a play at Shakespeare's theatre in Canterbury, and to enjoy more gatherings with family and friends. Lily informed Diana as a thank you that she would like to perform the concert she had been practicing. Diana asked Lily to play on their last night at the going away dinner party she was planning, if it would not be too tiring for her. Lily thought that was perfect. Lily needed a little more practice, but she would be ready.

A month before their departure, Lily and John took the train to London to visit Aunt Tess, Uncle Albert, and Bert, who were excited about their visit. They lived in a lovely brown stone townhouse in Mayfair. After unpacking and dressing for dinner, all met in the dining room. While eating, Aunt Tess listed what she planned. There would be sightseeing to Buckingham Palace, Parliament, Big Ben, Westminster Abbey, London Bridge, and the Victoria and Albert Museum with high tea. Shopping was a must at Selfridges, Fortnum and Mason, Hatchards Bookshop, Charbonnel et Walker for chocolates, Penhaligon's (known for "Hammam Bouquet" perfume around the world), and Harrods, which would include high tea. One night, they would enjoy fish and chips at the Andersons' favorite pub, then attend the production of Oscar Wilde's play, *The Importance of Being Earnest*. The second night was a symphony concert they thought Lily would enjoy. The third night revealed a dinner cruise along the Thames River with dinner music played by musicians. The evening would end with a spectacular show of fireworks from the paddle boat. The last night was a surprise attendance at the Gaiety Theatre. The theatre offered a new concept that everyone appeared to enjoy, with singing, dancing, comedy, and acting rolled into one. The combination was considered a vaudeville show from America. The last afternoon, Lily gave her concert to thank everyone for their hospitality and presented them with a basket full of goodies picked up from various shops in London. On the train ride back to Scotney Castle, she and John fell asleep from exhaustion. They did not know how his aunt and uncle endured the busy schedule his aunt had planned.

The next couple of weeks, the honeymooners took time to relax, play cards with his family, and had the chef write up the recipes they wanted to take back to Mario. Lily asked Lacy to play piano duets and sing with her. They had a great time. Diana's last night dinner party was a big success but did not top Lily's performance with Lacy singing "Amazing Grace." All of them suggested Lily perform on tour in England.

The next morning, the maid and groomsman packed their belongings and packages from shopping and ate breakfast with the family. They had had such a delightful time that they hated to leave. Lacy handed Lily a package with items precious to her that she felt Lily should have. There was a music box given to her by her husband as an engagement present, a cameo broach from her father, and her pearl necklace from her and her husband's twenty-fifth anniversary. These would always be treasured. Lily hugged Lacy and wished her well.

They promised to come back to visit after John's family came for a proper visit in America. After lunch, Lily and John took the train to Dover then boarded their ship. They felt sentimental as they sailed home. On the trip back, Lily was more relaxed and did practice three mornings for two hours. The honeymoon was perfect!

Chapter 26

They were approaching the dock. The honeymoon was over. They were a married couple who loved each other deeply. Violet and Ricardo met them at the dock. Lily was disappointed Lorenzo was not there to pick them up but understood his busy schedule. Violet inquired about their honeymoon and was pleased it all went so well. John thought his parents might retire here when he and Lily had children. Lily did not want them to give up their exquisite home.

Lily knew her mother. Something was not right. "How is Papa?"

"Lorenzo is not doing well. Be prepared. He naps a lot. Some days are good. He has cancer and does not want anyone to know yet. I had to pry it out of Sal. He was given two years. Please Lily, respect his request for privacy. This is his wish. He hates being pampered. We must keep everything normal. Sal is taking this awfully hard. They have been together for so long."

Violet remained quiet while Lily cried on John's shoulders. Just a few minutes before arriving, Lily wiped her tears and tried to look happy. They entered the penthouse where Lorenzo, Sal, and

Sonata were there to greet them. Lorenzo looked pale and thinner. He put on his beautiful smile just for her. She ran to him, hugged him, and kissed his cheek. “I missed you so much Papa!”

“I am sure the Anderson’s loved having you and kept you busy. It is good to have you home, Little Bird. We missed you, too,” said Lorenzo.

“They loved having her. She performed for them, and they think she should tour England,” John said with pride.

Lily went to Sal, hugged him, and kissed him hello. “I missed you, too, Uncle Sal.”

She turned to Lorenzo and said, “I am exhausted from the trip. If you will excuse me, I would like to lie down and take a quick nap before dinner. Which reminds me, John do not let me forget to give Mario those recipes at dinner.”

“I am sure you both are exhausted. I will see you at dinner. Welcome home, Little Bird. I hope you like your new room. Sing, Little Bird, sing. I love you,” he said rubbing her arm.

“I love you, too, Papa.”

The suite was decorated in blues and whites with accents in yellow. On a background of sky-blue wallpaper, branches of cherry blossoms appeared to pop off the sky. Here and there were tiny yellow birds with their mouths open as though they were singing. A matching bedspread accented the white bed with yellow throw pillows. Lily was overwhelmed by the family's thoughtfulness but also burdened by the shocking news of her Papa's health. Lily took off her shoes and got into bed. John lay next to her and secured his arms around her so that her face was cradled to his chest and his chin rested on her head. She cried herself to sleep in his arms.

They made day-to-day life as normal as possible. Lily was thankful Lorenzo was not needed for practice. Before the wedding, she had hired a black waitress who could sing opera but was not allowed to perform. Her name was Matilda Sissieretta Joyner Jones, but she went by Madame Jones. Lily hired her with lucrative pay. She made sure a large order of roses would be given to her at the end of her performance. Lily needed to take some time to adjust to everything at home again. The two would start to practice together in November for a few hours a week due to Madame Jones's work schedule. Lily had Ricardo pick Madame Jones up and drive her safely home after each practice. They would break for three weeks during Christmas and

New Year's Eve, which was Madame Jones' busiest work schedule, then start back up until three days before the concert. On those three days, they would practice diligently on stage.

Lily made sure she gave excuses of needing to practice or John planning something for them to do so that Lorenzo had more time to rest. Violet had written to all, so they were aware of what was transpiring but promised to keep silent. Christmas came, the family visited like always, and Lorenzo appeared to have more energy.

But before the family members left New York, Lorenzo gathered everyone to let them know he had only six months to live. He promised that they would all be taken care of because they had taken such wonderful care of him. He thanked them in a most sincere, sentimental voice. They meant a lot to him. Every member hugged him and said they were sorry to hear such bad news.

Once all of them had calmed down, Lily got up and asked for their attention for a moment. She felt this was the right time to give everyone something to happily anticipate, especially Lorenzo. "John and I have good news. We will be having a baby in about six or seven months." Everyone hugged the happy couple.

"I hope I get to see my grandchild before I go," expressed a tearful Lorenzo.

"I know you will be here for the occasion," replied Lily as she hugged him.

Everyone left with bad and good news, unsure what the new year had in store for them.

Every night, Lorenzo still rubbed Lily's arm and said, "Sing, Little Bird, sing. I love you."

Lily responded each time, "I love you too, Papa."

They would hug and Lorenzo would kiss the top of her head. Sal and James would help him to bed.

Every night, Sal reassured Lorenzo he had no regrets about coming to America with him. Theirs was the greatest adventure anyone could have and the greatest love, one never to forget.

Chapter 27

The next two months, Sal, James, Ricardo, Jasper, and John took turns taking care of Lorenzo. He was declining. Even Sonata appeared to be aware of Lorenzo's condition and would not leave his side except for walks and meals. Lorenzo loved to pet Sonata's soft fur. The kind animal relaxed him. When the family arrived from Georgia before the concert, they were quiet and knew the routine. The day of the concert, Lorenzo appeared to have gotten some strength but still needed assistance. Everyone cheered up when they sensed his newfound energy.

John would announce Lily and her program. In the booth, Lorenzo sat between Sal and Violet, along with Ida and Carolyn. Tom, Duncan, and James sat in the second row. Chairs made up a third row for Ricardo, Jasper, Mario, and Adele. The Marys could not attend the performance.

John walked onto the center of the stage and began speaking, "Good evening, ladies and gentlemen. I want you to know this is Lily Tucci's last performance for a while." The audience moaned. "She is taking time off to have our baby."

Everyone applauded. "Thank you. Tonight's performance will start with Pachelbel's "Canon in

D," followed by John Newton's "Amazing Grace" with a special performance by Madame Jones, and a finale by Lily Tucci called "Sing, Little Bird, Sing," which she dedicates to her Papa, Lorenzo Tucci. I give you Lily Tucci."

The audience applauded as Lily came on stage. She bowed then sat. They loved "Canon in D." She held her breath as John escorted Madame Jones to the front of the piano. Whispers were heard. Some people left, acting as though they were disgusted. Both women held their heads high and began. Those who did not leave enjoyed an unforgettable performance. Everyone stood and applauded wildly. There was not a dry eye in the house. John handed the roses to Madame Jones. She bowed, then John escorted her off the stage. Theirs was the only theatre ever to allow her to perform.

Next, Lily took a deep breath and played. She started her storm and chirps, building to the great storm then transitioning to the frolicking melody with more chirps followed by the tranquil melody with upper keys in song. Then, she played her finale with right fingers quickly gliding across only the upper keys. The audience stood and applauded. Many audience members whistled. Her piece was a hit.

Lorenzo turned to Violet and spoke softly, "I loved it. I am so proud of her. My Little Bird sang and now has taken flight." Then, quickly, his head fell forward. He had flown, too. While everyone was standing and applauding, Ricardo and James took Lorenzo back to his bed. They would call the doctor and undertaker. Sal was to take all to the party and be Lorenzo's spokesperson for the evening. He would be there for Lily in Lorenzo's place.

At the party, Sal told Lily that Lorenzo had become tired but wanted her to know how much he loved her composition. He told her, "Lorenzo said, 'My Little Bird sang and now has taken flight.'" Lily teared up from the special thought. She would talk to him tomorrow after he rested. That appeased her and she began to enjoy the party. The evening ended, and family members returned to the penthouse.

Sal, Tom, John, and Violet escorted Lily into the parlor and sat her down. John knelt before Lily and held her hands, "My love, Lorenzo passed away after the concert. He was able to hear everything. He was immensely proud that you had Madame Jones sing. He loved your composition for him. As Sal told you, Lorenzo said you sang and now have taken flight."

Lily cried into John's arms then looked at Sal. "Oh, Uncle Sal, what will we do without him?"

"Live together as a family, do for others, and love. I love you too, Little Bird. We will discuss it all tomorrow. We all need to get some sleep, especially you with the baby. You will need your strength for the next couple of days. John, please escort her to your room and watch over her tonight."

"Thank you, Uncle Sal. I love you, too. I am your Little Bird now." She hugged and kissed Uncle Sal.

John picked her up and carried her to bed.

Everyone left the parlor except Sal. He poured himself a stiff drink and sat in Lorenzo's favorite leather chair by the fireplace. A fire was still blazing, keeping the room warm. He took a couple of sips, then thought. He had to be strong for everyone right now. He could mourn after everyone left. His love just died. All those wonderful years together. He would never forget or regret. He wondered if the Marys had discovered the secret passage between their bedrooms. Oh, those nightly rendezvous! of stolen kisses in the office, elevator, or terrace. They had a long life together, more than most. So many memories made here. How could he live here now? Ida and Duncan offered to have him come live with them. He would be close to Lily and her family but have the quiet farm life. They had his own suite downstairs. He and Duncan got along splendidly. Sports were big in Georgia, too. It was time for him to retire and enjoy life. Before Ida and Duncan left, he would let them know he would graciously accept with conditions on helping. He would settle the estate then sell the penthouse if Lily was not going to stay. When all was settled, he would move. He was thankful for the two new assistants and John. They would help with the funeral plans Lorenzo requested and the transition of the company before he retired. He finished his drink then went to bed.

Chapter 28

Sal went through the funeral plans. Everyone was in town, so the service would take place tomorrow at 10:00 AM. The announcement went to the paper last night and would be in today's paper. A horse drawn carriage would bring the casket to the crypt at the local cemetery. There, a short ceremony would take place. Several people requested to sing some of Lorenzo's favorite songs, and Duncan would play "Amazing Grace" on the bagpipes. The minister had been instructed to keep the service short. After, all would be invited to Antonio's for lunch.

There were over one hundred people in attendance. Not all came to Antonio's. No one ate much, so Antonio and Rosa boxed up the leftovers so that Mario did not have to cook for a couple of days. The family stayed in New York a while longer to ensure Lily, Violet, and Sal were okay.

Sal had Lily, Violet, and John come to his office. "I will be retiring after Lorenzo's estate is completely settled. Lily, will you be staying in the penthouse?"

"No, Uncle Sal. John and I discussed that with Lorenzo gone, I would like to move back to Georgia. There are too many memories of him here. Aunt Carolyn and Uncle Tom have invited us to stay with them. Uncle Tom will be opening another law office in Atlanta and has asked John to partner with him. Uncle Tom is finding property for us in the western part of Atlanta. Once we build a home, we would love for you to live with us."

"I would love that, but Ida and Duncan have offered to have me stay with them, and I have accepted. I will be close by to enjoy you and your family for holidays, birthdays, picnics, and meals. I enjoy children, but being older, I need my quiet space. Once the estate is settled and an office is set up for the company, I will sell the penthouse and move to Georgia. Hopefully, I will be in Georgia before the baby is born!"

Lily got up and hugged Uncle Sal. "That would be wonderful."

"Violet, as his sister, he has left you $500,000 to do with as you wish. Lily, he has left you his entire estate and money minus the funds for his charities and projects stated. John, you are to be Lily's counselor and advisor and the president of the company. You are well versed in everything and will do a great job. I will be available if you ever need consultation. A current project is contracted with Frank Damrosch, grandson of Liszt, who is an English professor here in the states. They were to start a school in two years for gifted artists and call it The Juilliard School. Lily, you will be in Georgia, so it would be inconvenient to teach at the school, but Lorenzo requested you be the head chairperson for the school. He wants you to hire the staff and board members and be head judge for admissions and competitions. John will have bi-yearly meetings in New York and a couple of other meetings, so Lily, you can schedule your trips with John's. That covers everything."

Lily went to Sal, "I am so glad you will be near us, Uncle Sal. You will have many more joyous years with all of us. We are a family! I'd like James, Mario, and Ricardo to come live with us once you sell the penthouse. Our house should be built by then. Jasper will not leave his family here, so he will not be coming with us."

"Do not worry. The guards, the Marys, and Adele will get severance pay that will set them up for life. As for Jasper, there are many wealthy people with unruly pets. I will set up his business and have a good kennel constructed. Word has spread how great he is with animals. Let us go talk to Ricardo, James, and Mario. I am sure that, as family members, they would love to go with you."

Epilogue

Five months later, Sal moved in with Ida and Duncan. They were happy for eight years until Sal passed away in his sleep. As requested, all brought him to rest next to Lorenzo in New York. In his formal kilt attire, Duncan played "Amazing Grace" on his bagpipes with tears streaming down his face. Tom, Jr., and Frank cried for their Uncle Sal. Lily and the women cried as well. They lunched at Antonio's but left for home immediately.

Sal left Ida and Duncan two million dollars as a thank you. They donated one and half million to a university in Atlanta to build a music building in honor of Salvadore De Marco. Lily donated Lorenzo's instruments and the second grand piano for students who could not afford to rent one. She thought Lorenzo would appreciate the gesture.

Tom opened a second law office in Atlanta and partnered with John. Carolyn and Tom built a four-bedroom house on six of the twenty acres Lily bought.

Tom, Jr., took over his father's position in the Macon office. He married his sweetheart and moved into the Harris's home in Macon.

Frank became a doctor in Atlanta. He married a nurse from the same hospital. They bought a house two blocks from the hospital.

Savanah got her wish. She married Jeffrey, who became the assistant manager for the train company in Macon. Savanah now teaches third grade in Macon. They moved into a two-story house at the end of Pecan Lane.

Lily and John built a three-bedroom cottage for his parents and grandmother on two of the acres they had purchased. They did not want to sell their estate in England. Their estate manager and son would run everything as usual and report to them monthly with a higher wage. Their thoughts were that the family could vacation there, or maybe someone in the family would take permanent residence in the castle. They rented out rooms and did special events for more income and to keep staff busy. They loved being with Lily, John, and family.

Lacy was able to enjoy Lily and the kids for four more years. As requested, Duncan played "Amazing Grace" for her funeral.

Lily and John built a six-bedroom Victorian home, a two-bedroom cottage for James and Mario, and a three-car garage with a two-bedroom apartment above for Ricardo on the rest of their property. Violet has her own suite on the first floor of the house next to the day nursery. Sonata, James, and Violet love watching the children for their parents. Lily and John have twin boys. They named them Lorenzo and Salvadore. The Andersons requested English names next—John III, nicknamed Johnny, or Elizabeth, nickname Lizzy. They got their wish. The following year Johnny arrived. Two years later, Lizzy arrived.

John aspires to be governor of Georgia. Lily teaches piano at the university, plays concerts at the university and in New York, plays concerts and judges for Juilliard, and enjoys her children and family.

Every Valentine's Day, all gather at Lily and John's house for spaghetti and meatballs, the special spread on Italian bread slices, tossed salad, and, of course, cannoli for dessert. After dinner, all gather in the living room where Lorenzo's grand piano takes the stage in a windowed circle corner built just for the instrument. On top sits a picture of Lorenzo, Sal, Violet, and Lily. Lily always plays "Swan Lake" (as a duet with Lacy when she was still alive) and then "Sing, Little Bird, Sing" for her Papa.

Family!

About the Author

Cindy M. Rankin was born and grew up in Illinois. She is a graduate of Northeastern Illinois University. She married Wayne in 1974.

They have a son, daughter, son-in-law, and two grandsons. They have lived in Illinois, Texas, Michigan, and Virginia, and now reside in Tennessee.

Cindy loves gardening, crocheting, hand quilting, cooking, traveling, baking, painting, games, watching movies, and writing books.

Twin Flame Trilogy was her first book. It was well received. Readers have been requesting a second book.

Cindy wrote a completely different storyline in *Sing, Little Bird, Sing,* her second novel. She loved the layers that developed through her story. The time period reflects the morals and social rules which make this story real. Madame Jones is real. She was considered better than the famous Italian opera singer at the time. Unfortunately, because she was black, she was not allowed to perform in public. Her performance with Lily never happened, but Cindy wanted to reflect Lily and Lorenzo's compassion for music and making things right. The relationship between Lorenzo and Sal was never acted upon in public or with family, as laws and the public did not condone homosexuality.

Cindy felt God, destiny, family, courage, and acceptance played a major part of this story. Cindy hopes you enjoy her books. Please let her know by writing reviews.

Discussion Questions

1. What if there were no family members to help this mother and daughter escape? What do you think they would have done? What other ways could they have escaped?

2. Did the officer recognize Lily but ignore her to keep them safe, or did Aunt Ida really change her look?

3. In today's society, would Lily be bullied? How might she be treated by family members, peers, and other musicians?

4. Was it God's plan or destiny behind Lily's journeys? Explain the miraculous and lucky moments in this story.

5. Would Sal and Lorenzo still hide their relationship in today's society?

6. In real life, Madame Jones did not sing at any concert halls due to her race. The author let her sing, but some audience members left in

disgust. Should the author have had most of the audience leave instead of only a few? Why?

7. Sal and Lorenzo did not pay to have George killed. What does that tell you about their character?

8. If you were to choose an alternate title to this book, what would you choose? Explain your decision.

9. What significance does Lacy play in the story?

10. What is the significance of Savanah at the close of the story, living in the house at the end of Pecan Lane?

11. How did listening to classical music on YouTube help you enjoy the book?

www.ingramcontent.com/pod-product-compliance
Lightning Source LLC
LaVergne TN
LVHW010659110826
845149LV00014B/3172